THROWING TARTS AT THE KING
AND OTHER STORIES

THROWING TARTS AT THE KING AND OTHER STORIES

ANNE BIANCO

This edition published in 2023
by Maida Vale Publishing,
An imprint of The Black Spring Press Group,
London, United Kingdom

Cover design by @padrondesign
Typeset by Subash Raghu

ISBN 978-1-913606-57-2

The author has requested American spelling and grammar be used for this book

For My Mother

ACKNOWLEDGEMENTS

I'd like to thank Erin McGraw for overseeing the inception of some of these stories years ago in a graduate workshop. For reading and invaluable comments, my heartfelt thanks go to Ginger Moran. For her care in editing, Dr. Memory Pinchbeck. Special thanks to Amira Ghanim who provided guidance throughout this process for which I'm grateful. I'd also like to thank Eyewear Publishing/Black Springs Press for this wonderful opportunity. Finally, and most of all, I'd like to thank my husband for his endless encouragement and support.

AUTHOR BIOGRAPHY

Anne grew up, the fourth of eight children, during the late sixties and seventies near Cleveland, Ohio. She developed an enduring love of literature and theater in elementary school. She graduated from Northwestern University and studied writing and education in graduate programs at the University of Cincinnati. She's lived in Chicago, rural Tennessee, and at present resides and writes in Cincinnati's Over-the-Rhine neighborhood with her husband and two beloved shelter dogs, Australian shepherds Gemma and Josie.

CONTENTS

THROWING TARTS AT THE KING

He hadn't ordered the torte or the petit fours. It was getting too hot to order the cheesecake topped with slices of kiwi, strawberries and peaches, or the chocolate cheesecake. He'd bent to eye the German chocolate cake, coconut visible in its frosting, and next to it, the orange fondant carrots atop cream cheese frosting on the carrot cake, but concluded that they might not hold up in the car. The tarts and cannolis were a smaller investment, probably still a mistake; but they might stay cool enough in the air conditioning to last for the ride. Still, he imagined what it would be like to make an entrance with a stack of boxes, "I had to get one of everything," to be so outrageously generous and thoughtful. Well, yes. These were the kinds of entrances Stash always made. Jack smiled. Then he frowned. Anyway, who could eat all of that? Who needed it? His mother didn't need to put on more weight, and his father had heart disease. Why help clog his arteries further? The tarts and cannolis were enough. A taste.

Already the skin on Jack's forearms reddened under the sunroof as he drove. The hell with it.

He tore the ribbon off one of the white boxes and opened it with his right hand, his left hand still on the steering wheel. The first tart was a cream tart, mocha cream, coffee-tainted, delicate buttery pastry topped with whipped cream and flecks of dark chocolate. Shavings they called them. Five more tarts and a half hour later, Jack realized, sleepily, he'd been unaware of his surroundings. He'd left the outskirts of the city and entered a countryside of vast green fields and farms. He opened the sunroof to snap out his stupor with a blast of fresh air, but after a minute the heat outside invaded the car and he couldn't feel the effects of the air conditioning. Muggy. He closed the sunroof again and ate two more tarts, key lime, very tangy. The other, he couldn't tell, coconut cream? The flavors had begun to taste the same: sweet. He didn't enjoy these as much as the first tarts. He tried to remember how many he'd eaten. He looked over at the open box on the passenger seat to count the remaining tarts, and glanced up just in time to jam on the brakes—he'd nearly rear-ended a semi. On the back of the silver truck, written in black script, the words, "The King." Silhouettes of reclining naked women faced each other from each mudflap. Bumper stickers read: "If you can read this you're too close,"

"When passing, please lift skirt," and "My son just beat up your honor student."

Jack switched into the left lane with a burst of acceleration. As he did, he noticed the truck signaling to move into the left lane as well, but Jack floored the engine and passed just as the truck maneuvered right behind him. Damn truck drivers. They did stuff like this all the time, on purpose. He sped ahead and switched back into the right lane. Again he opened the sunroof, feeling sweaty from the burst of adrenaline caused by his near collision, and set the cruise control at 75 mph. In the split second it took the cab section of the truck to pass him, Jack saw the driver lean forward and make some gesture, it looked more like a salute than the finger. Smart ass. Jack grabbed a tart, and it was awkward, but he stuck his hand out the open sunroof and threw the tart at the shimmering silver gray side of the truck. He heard a tiny thump as the tart landed on his own back window. He glanced in the rearview mirror and saw that the tart had blown away, leaving a pasty residue. As if to one up him, the truck signaled and changed lanes right in front of Jack, leaving him little following distance. This time Jack grabbed a handful of tarts. Using his left foot, he pushed his body higher up to get more leverage, stuck his hand back out the sunroof, aimed, and threw. The tarts hit the black script of "The King," but most of them disintegrated and fell back onto his windshield, unnoticed and soundless below the din of engines and the roar of air at high velocity. Jack swerved and regained control of the car, then slowed, allowing himself to fall far behind. His sticky right hand fumbled for the button to close the sunroof. Damn. Mocha cream all over his windshield. He squirted windshield wiper fluid and ran the wipers. Streams of milky cream oozed down and smeared a faint film all over the glass, clouding his vision. He worked the wiper fluid and blades furiously until he could see better. But he felt nauseous. He pulled over at the next exit and drove to a drive-thru to get some coffee.

He ordered a medium, black, and while he waited, remembered how his older brother, Stash, put a lot of milk in his coffee. Until it was spilling over onto a saucer. Or whatever surface he'd placed his mug on, whether a book, a table, the floor, so that rings from his coffee cups could still be found in various places all over the house long after Stash went away to college. "You want some coffee with your milk?" was the old joke. Then there was the time Stash managed to spill a whole half gallon carton of milk over his head at lunch. He sat blinking through the whiteness, then tasting the drops rolling down his nose in that way he had, smacking his lips and looking up at the ceiling, reflecting on the flavor. The tenderness this memory evoked in Jack surprised him. He found himself staring, as if he might cry, at the woman in the drive-thru window who held out his change. As he put his coffee in the cupholder, he sensed a heaviness in his bladder. Better use the restroom. He pulled over and parked. Out of the corner of his eye he saw a few trucks parked behind the Stuckey's in places reserved for them, and he thought he might have seen a man in a baseball cap, walking around to inspect his truck. Jack locked the car and looked again, but the man was gone.

He shrugged uneasily to himself and walked into the restaurant. He found the restroom empty, and leaned into the urinal with relief. He looked down into the rusty urinal hole and noticed the standard fast food red brick floors around it were damp and sticky with the piss of many travelers. Jack felt a wave of nausea, and stifled a gag. The air smelled of urine and heavy institutional cleaners used to deaden the stench. He straightened up, then leaned for a moment against the brick wall of the restroom, and the nausea passed. He washed his hands and used a towel to dab at the sweat on his forehead. Then he went back to the parking lot.

Outside the trucker was walking around his car, scratching his chin, a cigarette lodged in his lips. Jack turned around, went back into the restroom, and threw up into the urinal. There. Much better. Maybe the trucker had gone now. He washed and dried his hands again and rubbed them together as if warming them before a campfire. His insides rumbled.

As he straightened up to look in the mirror, the trucker in the baseball cap pushed through the restroom door. Jack swabbed at his mouth with a paper towel as the trucker peed. He was about to make his escape when the trucker spoke.

"What in the Lord's hell is that?"

Jack pretended not to hear, pushed open the door and started out.

"Hey you."

Jack turned slowly to face the man.

"You see that?" The trucker zipped his pants and nodded downward to the offending urinal.

"What." Jack squinted at the urinal.

"Somebody puked in there and just left it."

"That's disgusting."

"Funny thing is," the truck driver said, "it looks like what I just saw on your car. Hey, buddy, you got a mess on your car. Some kinda...shit on your windshield."

Jack tried to leave but the trucker stopped him, his grip tight on his wrist.

"You having a *problem* today, boy?" The trucker shoved his face close to Jack's and looked him in the eyes. His breath smelled of tobacco and coffee, and for a moment Jack was reminded of his grade school teachers at St. Patrick's. Without his sunglasses, the skin around the trucker's eyes looked cool and pale and vulnerable as the underside of a lizard. Wiry, with reddish brown hair, hazel eyes, and a bushy mustache, all under a black CAT baseball cap.

Yosemite Sam, Jack thought, but knew enough not to say so. His eyes hurt to stare at the man at such close range, so he glanced at his t-shirt, which read, "Not listening." Jack shrugged, tried to keep the corners of his mouth from turning up in a nervous smile.

"Something funny?"

Jack really didn't expect the blow to his stomach. He crumpled to the floor along the wall of the restroom, whispered, "Ouch," indignantly. His breath came in short gasps. He was also surprised that it didn't hurt that badly. He found himself smiling from his seat on the sticky tile. The trucker kicked his right arm.

"Don't you know I can see everything from my rig? Why did you throw shit at my truck?"

★★★★★

Stash lay on the living room couch, sick with the flu. Jack was going to do Stash's newspaper route for the first time alone. With the large blue canvas newspaper bag slung over his shoulder, Jack rode his yellow banana seat bicycle the ten blocks to Birdtown, where the streets were named Oriole, Thrush, and Lark. Yackshimash Town, they called it because the language of the Slovak people living in Birdtown sounded like "Yackshimash" to them. Jack parked his bike on the sidewalk and went up crumbling driveways to put newspapers in milk chutes or side doors. He threw some up onto porches, took one directly to the rectory of the Slovenian church. At the last house on the route, the customer wanted the newspaper put inside the screen door on the front porch. Jack climbed the steps and hesitated when he heard a dog growling inside. He was about to open the door, throw the paper in and run away, when an old woman opened the inner, heavy wooden door and peered out at him from the darkness inside, her head wrapped in a bubushka, her eyes black and piercing as Jack's rosary beads.

'Ver is old newspaper boy?" she asked suspiciously, her dog yelping and scratching at the screen. She looked Jack up and down.

"He's sick. I'm his brother," Jack answered, holding out the folded evening paper.

The old woman cracked the screen door open a few inches and grabbed it.

"Old newspaper boy is best newspaper boy we efer haf." She slammed the wooden door shut.

"They like you once they get to know you," Stash explained later.

Birdtown was a block away from Madison Park, where Stash and Jack went swimming in the summer at the community pool. Stash performed scary jumps, sailor's dives, suicides, and cannonballs off the high board. One July day as Jack sat on a bench, facing the diving boards wrapped in the new towel Stash had given him for his birthday, his older brother ran up to him and asked, "Wanna see a big splash?"

Stash ran around the pool and waited his turn before climbing the high board. His brother's dark head appeared first, hair wet and flattened against his skull, and then the rest of him materialized at the top of the steps against a seamless, clear blue sky. Stash stood for a moment at the far end of the board, focusing. Then he ran out, bounced once, flew into the air, grabbed his knee and leaned backwards, executing a perfect can opener, before landing in the water and producing what Jack and everyone else watching felt was almost a sonic boom. Water could be heard splatting down on the pavement of the pool deck in a radius of five feet as watchers oohed and aahed. A few boos and hisses came from the Canarvous gang. A pack of lean tanned leathery brown teenagers, sitting on their towels in a corner near the chain link fence. Stash's head popped up slick as a seal's from under blue-green water near the ladder. He climbed out, dripping and shaking water from his ears.

Later, when it was time for Jack to go home and for Stash to do his paper route, Jack couldn't find his new red, white, and blue striped beach towel. He looked all around the pool, and finally came upon Nicky Canarvous, sitting on his towel by the chain link fence.

"That's my towel."

"Why dontcha go get your big brother, dickface. He's the one with the nice bike, right?" Nicky laughed.

Jack ran to find Stash, but a lifeguard hooted "Young man, walk!" through her megaphone, so he slowed down. He found Stash talking to Janis, the prettiest girl at the pool. She wore a hot pink bikini and had a perfect tan.

"Canarvous has my towel," he gasped. The sun had already dried his skin, and he felt its tightness and the tiredness in his body from an afternoon of swimming.

Stash looked over to where Canarvous sat. He turned and smiled at Janis, and without a word, walked over to confront Nicky, Jack following close behind. But when they came closer, Jack saw that his towel was gone.

"What." Canarvous shielded his eyes from the glare, looked up at Stash.

Stash shook his head. "Give him his towel, Canarvous."

"I don't got it." Incredulous to be so accused.

"Stash, he did, he did."

"Come on Canarvous. Just give it back."

"Can't give it back if I don't got it."

What could they do? Another time, Stash's new ten speed bike, bought with his newspaper route money, disappeared from the pool bike rack where he'd locked it with a strong, expensive lock, and no one ever found out who stole it, but they guessed it must have been Nicky, too. Luckily, he'd bought insurance. That's how smart Stash was. He thought ahead about things like that.

The last time Jack saw Stash was a year ago, at their sister's wedding rehearsal dinner. The event was held at a seafood restaurant down in the Cleveland Flats on the Cuyahoga River, beneath towering black bridges that rose and fell for tugboats. Stash arrived late into the meal with his current girlfriend, Susan, who was five months pregnant. Jack guessed Susan to be about thirty. She had a beautiful, Asian-American face, though Jack didn't know and couldn't tell if she was Japanese or Hawaiian. Susan was petite, with long, glossy black hair that hung to her behind. Her belly had begun to show under a long silk tunic and baggy silk pants. Definitely a Stash woman, but what Jack remembered most was Susan's voice, which was girlish and coaxing.

"Well, Jack, aren't you going to introduce me?" she asked after dinner as Jack talked with a cousin from New Jersey who knew nothing of Susan's pregnancy, or even who she was. She took Jack's arm, tossed some of her abundant hair back, and beamed at both of them warmly. Confused, Jack blushed and stammered.

"Susan, this is my cousin Donna, my Dad's brother's daughter. Donna, this is Stash's girlfriend Susan." He couldn't say fiancée. He'd only learned that morning about her pregnancy, and only by looking at her. Stash hadn't said a thing, nor had he told anyone of their plans, or even if they had any.

Donna smiled and said hello, but Susan's eyes narrowed, her jaw stiffened, and for a moment Jack thought he glimpsed an angry mask. But she quickly recovered her pleasing demeanor.

"I'm not just his girlfriend, I'm going to have his baby." As if Jack had deprived her of a title she deserved.

I'm going to have his baby! It sounded like...like a horrible soap opera!

"Oh," Donna said, and her tone was sincere, if surprised. "Congratulations!"

Jack walked away in a daze to order another drink at the bar. He stared, unseeing, at his reflection in the mirror behind all the bottles of liquor. Stash appeared next to him in the reflection. Jack turned to face him, his older, taller, always praised, better-looking and more successful brother. Today Stash's face had a puffy look, as if he retained water or had been eating too many rich foods and not working out. His black suit trousers looked snug at the waist. His moist, blood-shot eyes stared down at Jack, penitent, trapped, lost.

"Hi, Stash." Think you're smart now, hot shit? Don Juan?

"I'm going to buy a house," Stash said.

"Yeah? Where?"

"It's going to be all right. It's not a mistake. She's the one, man."

"You'll be a great father," Jack said, and meant it. He swallowed the rest of his drink in one gulp.

Stash bowed his head and looked the six feet down to his well-worn olive green and cream colored snake-skin cowboy boots. Jack felt sudden remorse for his lack of words, his lack of empathy. But it wasn't lack of empathy! He'd had enough of Stash and his reign as the best and brightest, and his family's denial of his imperfections. This was not envy!

Susan snuck up behind Stash then, gesturing at Jack not to give her away. Her arms undulated like snakes as she prepared to either blindfold or hug him from behind, Jack didn't know. He envisioned Susan's hair rising into the air like tentacles, strangling Stash instead. At the same time, her swollen belly drew his gaze.

"Guess who?"

"I don't know," Stash played along. He sounded tired. His lips curled into an irritated smile, but he humored Susan like a child.

"Me!" she cried, hopping around in front of Stash and hugging him. "I'm so lucky to have met your brother, Jack!"

I know *you* are, he thought.

Stash sighed. "We've got to go. We'll see you at the wedding tomorrow.

Jack stared through Stash as if he were a ghost. Then Stash did something he'd never, ever done before. He bent over and kissed Jack on his head, on his hair, and Jack didn't feel foolish. He didn't know what it meant until a month later when Stash died after going under a truck in his car at upwards of 80 mph. Stash had been kissing him goodbye. But no. He couldn't have known, could he?

★★★★★

Jack rubbed his arm and looked up at the trucker standing over him.

"Maybe because you changed lanes on purpose to annoy the hell out of me when I tried to pass. I mean, why do you guys always do that? I was trying to pass, you pull out. Where was I supposed to go, off the road?"

The trucker looked up and around the restroom. Jack felt like saying, as his elementary teachers used to, "You won't find the answer on the ceiling…" The trucker opened and closed his mouth a few times, working his mustache up and down like a scrub brush.

"I didn't see you," he said finally.

"I thought you could see everything. Anyway, it's a good day to die I guess." Jack's lips quivered a little, and his voice shook. Pathetic, too, on the scummy floor of a truckstop pisser. At least Stash died going fast. He probably didn't feel much. Neither way was heroic, he supposed. He felt a pain in his lower left back and felt sorry for himself.

The trucker's eyes widened. He laughed a low, raspy chuckle. "It sure as hell is, you sorry sack a shit!" He pulled a cigarette out of his shirt pocket and a lighter out of the back pocket of his jeans.

"You got that right." Jack smoothed his white tennis shirt. "Can I go now or are you going to kill me first?" He tried to sound cavalier, but felt like he might throw up again. He stood slowly, rubbing his gut.

Another smile began on the trucker's lips, sending his mustache all the way up to the high cheekbones under his sunken eyes. "Smoke?"

"No thanks." Jack realized the situation was scarier than anything that had ever happened or that he'd done in his life, including taking the bar exam, but it occurred to him that even though he'd done everything expected of him, he wasn't happy. He felt like he'd missed out on something, and was filled with a sense of regret and recklessness that raised the hair on the back of his neck. He felt strong! What did it feel like to…

Jack aimed for the trucker's nose but succeeded in punching him on his right cheek, sending his baseball cap flying. There. Surprise registered on both of their faces as the man fell back against the sink, his keychain jangling.

"You're gonna be sorry you were ever born, boy!" The trucker lunged at Jack, bloodying his nose and dragging him back to the floor.

"I already am," Jack hissed, holding the trucker by his hair as he slammed Jack's head on the dirty tile two or three times before, gasping, the trucker let go and sat up under the sink.

"I'm too old for this. I got fifteen years on you at least," the man said. He touched his cheek and winced.

Jack sniffed, wiping his nose with his shirt. For a moment they stared at each other.

Then the trucker chuckled and lit another cigarette. "Look, I'm sorry I got in your face. It's just, no one touches The King. That's what I call my rig."

"I know. I saw."

"I don't even let my kids in the cab." The trucker shrugged, pulling himself slowly to his feet. "Name's Larry Buford. You're a mess. Let me buy you a cup of coffee."

Still wary of the man's boots, Jack struggled to stand. "Jack Osinski," he said finally, offering his hand. "Thanks, but I already had some coffee."

"What was it you threw at my truck?"

"Tarts." Jack's body felt like it did after he ran a marathon, sore in every joint.

"Tarts. Bakery tarts?"

"Yeah. You want some? I have a whole other box in my car."

"No, no. You keep your tarts. Where you going, a piano recital?"

"Home."

"Home? Didn't anyone ever tell you, you can't go home again?"

★★★★★★

Jack started his car and glanced over at the untouched box of tarts. That morning, before he'd risen early to run, he awoke from a dream where he stood on the altar of St. Patrick's Church, his arms raised as if to conjure Stash up and out of his coffin. Arise!

Stash sat up, fell out of the coffin, then climbed back in and was quiet again.

"Hey! I want to talk to you!" Jack shouted, but Stash didn't answer.

Driving out of the parking lot, Jack rolled to a stop near The King, white hot and glinting in the sunlight like a great monument. He looked back toward the restaurant and saw Larry Buford in his black cap, inside the diner, watching him. The King's windows were closed tight, and Jack was sure the doors were locked, too.

STONE'S THROW

Tom struggled to keep up with Frank's buoyant pace. His brother walked shoulders hunched forward, gloveless hands jammed into the pockets of his peacoat, down Sixth Street to Monmouth, where the movie theater marquee announced a Sunday matinee episode of Rin Tin Tin. Earlier that winter Frank had walked on the frozen Ohio River. The ice that trapped the Island Queen at Cincinnati's Public Landing had long since thawed. Even now, sunlight reduced the morning's freezing drizzle to tendrils of steam rising from the pavement, but snow still lingered on sidewalks and lawns. Tom's wool cap nearly covered his eyes, forcing him to look down at his feet as he walked. When Frank suddenly stopped at the corner, Tom bumped into him.

"Sorry," he said.

Frank smiled and looked down the Roman nose chiseled into his thirteen-year-old face, considering Tom as if he'd forgotten him. Then he turned and crossed Monmouth north to Fifth and continued on Fifth to York where they spotted Little Manny bouncing a rubber ball as hard and high as he could muster; then catching it, on the sidewalk in front of the courthouse.

"Brought the punk, Frankie?"

Frank shrugged.

"We're goin' to the movie," Tom offered.

Little Manny grinned. "What I tell you?" he asked his ball before putting it in his coat pocket. He snorted and blew a wad of spit all the way to the street. Short and stocky with a mass of shiny black curls, his dad, Big Manny, worked in a coal mine down in Hazard.

"Wanna skip stones, Tommy?" Frank asked.

"Sure!"

"We'll let you skip stones wit' us, you don't tell your mama," said Little Manny.

"Let's go to Covington, it ain't that far," Frank reasoned, pointing to the bridge across the Licking.

"Oh, I get it." Little Manny stooped, pretended to walk with a cane, and affected an old man's reedy voice. "Grandpa Vic is taking his Sunday institutional (sic) down the Port of Entry, and you're supposed to be at the movies, right?"

They laughed, then he and little Manny continued walking down Fourth toward the bridge. Tom jogged slowly to keep up.

Once across they turned right on Garrard Street and scrambled down the bank. The muddy river moved steadily southwestward with a low, murmuring hiss. Its current swirled around a large black rock ten feet from the bank.

Frank picked up a thin piece of shale. "Find one like this," he said, showing Tom. "Hold it level."

He moved up the bank a few feet and drew his arm back. With the momentum of a few steps toward the water and a flick of his wrist, Frank threw the stone. The shale skimmed the moving surface of the river six times before disappearing. How long before it hit bottom? Tom looked across the river at the Queen City Paper sign.

"I bet you could skip one all the way across, Frank!" he yelled.

Tom looked around for his own skipping stone while Frank walked further down the bank with Little Manny. Mist enveloped the suspension bridge and rolled out over the brown water like steam on hot chocolate. A red tug prodded a coal barge upstream against the current, which churned in protest. Frank and Little Manny's voices seemed to float to Tom from far away. Glancing toward the sound, their figures disappeared and reappeared in the fog.

Tom spotted a gray-green wedge of shale. Grunting, he bent down to pick up the stone. Wrapped up in hat and scarf, he could hear himself breathing heavily. It was delightful to see his breath emerge as steam, almost touchable. He trudged back down to the water, clutching the stone in his gloved hand.

"Look, Tommy!" Frank yelled. Little Manny held up a dead fish on a stick. Tom grinned and waved. When he took a step forward, his right foot sunk into what looked like solid ground but was actually mud that gave way to a foot of water. He staggered, lost his balance, and plunged forward into the river.

The first time he went under he was mostly surprised, waiting for his feet to hit a bottom that never arrived. In seconds the cold shock of water soaked his wool coat and carried his hat away. He struggled to move his arms.

The second time, he swallowed a mouthful of water that tasted of snow and dirt. He choked, inhaling more. His rubber boots were heavy weights pulling him down. The third time he went under he thought *This is it* and began to pray. He heard Frank and Little Manny yelling, and stopped struggling a moment to listen. The current carried him around the big rock and back toward the bank where Frank held the stick out over the water. Gasping, Tom grabbed it, and together Manny and Frank dragged him out of the river.

At home Frank tried to sneak Tom past the kitchen and upstairs through the back door, but Ma saw them. Her smile faded to a frown, her eyes narrowed in shock and horror. Tom's teeth chattered so badly he couldn't speak. Frank tried to explain but Ma didn't listen. She dragged them both through the swinging doors into the restaurant where Pop took one look at Tom and came charging at Frank from behind the bar.

"What did I tell you?" he shouted. "Going to the movies." Glasses rattled. Jars of mozzarella in olive oil and bottles of wine shook on their shelves as Pop chased Frank and caught him. Tom heard a slap, then nothing. Frank never cried, ever. Mama stripped Tom of his wet clothes and wrapped him, shivering uncontrollably, in blankets.

Late that night something woke Tom from a dream of Frank walking on the frozen river, of ice breaking away and carrying his brother downstream. He looked up to find the familiar outlines of baseball pennants on the walls, the wooden crucifix with a sliding panel that held Last Rites holy water and candles—he was home, in the bedroom he shared with his brother. The sound of a stifled sob from Frank's bed made him sit up.

"Frank?" he whispered. His head hurt, his tongue felt swollen. "I wanted to tell them it wasn't your fault but I couldn't talk."

Had he actually spoken? Frank lay so still he appeared to have stopped breathing.

"Frank?"

Sometimes when he closed his eyes he felt the smooth sensation of water running through his fingers. Sometimes the water became shards of ice that scratched his hands. Voices were either as loud as thunder or so quiet he couldn't hear them. Dr. Gray listened to his heart. Ma hovered, dabbing his head with cool washcloths. Frank left in the morning and returned in the evening without a word.

When Tom woke on his first day back at school, Frank's bed was already made. A river tug's horn sounded muffled as if...Tom wiped his foggy window and looked out to see snow had fallen overnight. He heard the back door slam shut downstairs.

In class that day they learned about the Ice Age. Did they know glaciers left behind erratic rock formations in the Kentucky woods nearby? Walking home, the bright sunlight and white snow blinded Tom and forced him to squint. He didn't know what hit him when an iceball smacked the back of his head, knocking his cap to the sidewalk. Turning around, another hit him in the jaw and brought tears to his eyes.

"All better, Tommy?" Little Manny grabbed his bookbag and hurled it toward the street. Tom's eyes followed the bookbag, which landed in a pile of gray slush amassed along the curb – at Frank's feet! Tom looked up at his brother and smiled, his heart pounding with relief, but Frank stood, his arms crossed, his face expressionless.

Little Manny gave him five seconds running before he tackled him and stuffed snow down his back. Their laughter faded away. Tom didn't have to look up to know his brother was gone.

He ran to the woods. He climbed over splintering tree roots and moss growing in crevices to the top of their favorite rock where he found his name and the date, 1939, etched into a corner overlooking the forest. Next to his, Frank's name painstakingly carved into the blue-black stone last summer. Maybe this rock was left behind by glaciers. It did seem odd, the way it rested precariously along a slope with no other rocks like it around.

Tom lay down flat on his stomach, arms out-stretched, hugging the rock. He pressed his cheek next to his brother's name where the stone felt warm. He could think of no reason for what had happened. No plan behind the movement of rivers, ice, stones, brother. He listened to his own breathing, to wind that rustled the dry dead leaves high in the trees while his tears wet the rock. All the same thing.

The air smelled of rain and thawing mud. Like spring.

This is it, he thought.

REPTILE ROUNDUP

Bernie Norman, eyes shining like pieces of iridescent metal, swept the rough gray conglomerate behind the garbage truck with his wooden push broom. To avoid the thought and consequent nausea of accidentally inhaling or swallowing one of the hovering black flies, he kept his mouth clamped shut in a grim line. The muscles in his moonlike face weren't accustomed to frowning and so this effort required some exertion. But if he smiled, his mouth cracked open, lips parted over a set of white teeth, uniform as corn kernels, and he quickly closed it again. Hap, who didn't seem to mind the flies that lit and crawled on him, pressed the red button and sent the hopper into a wail. Bernie held his breath, scrunching up his nose as if to close his nostrils. More flies and the sweetish smell of decaying produce wafted back at them from the air smashed out of compressed refuse.

"Lunchtime." Hap heaved his green barrel into the back. A blue Buick rolled to a stop behind the truck. Without turning around, Hap waved impatiently to the driver with his lean, bare arm to just go ahead and pass. The Buick, or the driver behind closed tinted windows hesitated, afraid to collide with unseen, oncoming traffic. The car's air conditioner hummed and whined alternately.

"Don't be an asshole," Hap muttered loudly to the car in the delirious heat. Still the Buick didn't move. Hap shook his head. White splotches appeared on his reddened face. Furious with the driver's indecision he motioned more vigorously with his left arm, strutting in his cutoff shorts to the garbage truck's driver's side door, and climbed in, slamming it. As the Buick passed cautiously, Bernie held his broom under one arm and grasped the long metal bar on the side of the hopper. He lifted one large foot clad in a heavy yellow boot with a sole like a bulldozer tread, clodhoppers, his old man called them, to the sideboard and hoisted himself up. The back of the truck sagged under his weight, the signal for Hap to hit the gas. Bernie's massive chest in a Spruce Grove Refuse shirt rose and fell. Lately he'd noticed his stomach, like rising bread dough, had begun to venture even further over the belt of his pants. The truck moaned down the street, Bernie swinging in the breeze like a friendly-faced, anchored zeppelin, waving to children drawing on the sidewalk with chalk.

"Bernie, Bernie," they cried, running after the truck. Sometimes he threw candy, careful not to throw any into the street where the children might get hurt. When Hap wasn't looking, if Hap had gone into a backyard, Bernie might hold one small child up to press the red button.

That job with Hap was his day job. Nights Bernie worked as a security guard at the Zoo.

"Why you wanna do two lousy jobs?" Hap asked as they ate lunch on a bench under some shady trees in the Spruce Grove suburban square. He bit into his sub sandwich and threw his head back to swallow. Sometimes Bernie worried about Hap. His face looked pretty red.

"It's a little more money, I pay Ma rent with it."

"That metal's gonna melt out here today," Hap said. Sculptures of American soldiers from every war, frozen in a bronze struggle to support the U.S. flag, stood as a centerpiece. The red brick pavers lent a colonial cobblestone formality to the sidewalk in this town where Bernie and Hap had grown up. Before it was a suburban town square and still part cornfield. Then came the development boom of the eighties, the state's biggest mall down the road, better public schools and mammoth new homes.

"You gotta take it easy, Hap. Too much with the hmm and the hmm of nights," and here Bernie mimed sipping beer and smoking cigarettes. "Get some exercise, give your body a break, you'd be a different person."

Hap sat up suddenly, his eyebrows rose, rippling the peeling skin on his sunburnt forehead.

"Don't start with me, Bernie," he said. "Too much with the…" and Hap pointed to his mouth and pretended to chew, exaggeratedly puffing out his cheeks. "Where do you get off? I mean, when do you even find the time to eat, Bernie, so much, working two jobs. You keep eatin' like that you're gonna be one dead sonofabitch of a heart attack age 35."

Bernie looked down at his lunch. He'd already finished the egg salad on wheat, but two sandwiches wrapped in wax paper remained: a turkey and Swiss on rye, and salami and provolone on Italian bread from the Spruce Grove Deli. As far as he was concerned, Bernie was glad all these upscale types had moved to Spruce Grove in suburban Cincinnati. They knew their food. It signified progress, despite what the old timers thought about higher taxes.

"I'm gonna start workin' out," Bernie resolved.

Hap snorted, nodding, "Yeah yeah yeah, that's what you always say."

"This time I mean it."

"When? You work day and night."

"I'll find a way. The Rec Center. City employees get a discount."

"Ha! They'll laugh you outta there, Bern. All those frat boys and skinny-assed moms in tights. People like us don't belong there." Hap stopped chewing. "Hey, you think I could go? Be your support system, like, spot you with weights? Your trainer. I'll say I'm your trainer." Hap laughed, cracked a soda, emptied it into his mouth and crushed the can in his fist.

The cool dusk at the Zoo afforded some relief from the day's heat even if a light breeze carried to Bernie's nostrils the smell of animal feces, cat urine, and fetid hot dogs in dumpsters. He reminded himself: here he was not a garbage man, and shouldn't think like one. But smells bothered him. He checked his appearance in the men's room mirror. Drooping hound dog brown eyes looked back at him. Al Pacino. *Say hello to my little friend.* Bernie sneered at himself, lips curling, and almost flinched at how menacing he suddenly looked.

Patrolling the grounds, his baton and flashlight swung from one hip, radio and keys bulged off the other. His radio beeped.

"Yeah."

"Hey, it's Grounds. Can you unlock the Nocturnal House?"

"Sure. What for?"

"That Reptile Roundup class, they're waiting outside to see the Komodo dragon."

"Be right there."

He strode across the zoo, past the gibbons, the elephants, and Monkey Island to the Nocturnal House, and spotted the class leader by her khaki Zoo uniform. She looked to be a young woman, 30, maybe younger, with shoulder length light brown hair and wide set brown eyes. He'd seen her before somewhere. Yes, teaching a class in the Owl Education Center. He recalled looking into a classroom to see her showing some children and their parents a turtle, which, Bernie remembered, had left a little doo-doo on the floor. A giftie. The children screamed with laughter. Turtle shit. He'd told Hap about it and Hap had laughed, as he always did about any kind of toilet humor. Her behind had some pizzazz, Bernie remembered. Definitely not a skinny-assed chick. It resembled one of those, what were they called? Bustles, from the old days, and was somehow comforting, easy on the eyes. Bernie smiled and nodded to her.

"Oh, great," she cried. Parents and children cleared a path for Bernie to the brown cedar door. Some of the teenagers, in heavy metal t-shirts or sporting blue hair, squashed themselves up against the handicap ramp's black railing as he passed. Searching for the correct key from about a hundred on his ring, Bernie smiled to himself, and then frowned, because for a moment he felt like Uncle Jingaling, that TV clown from his childhood. Given the chance to be on Uncle Jingaling's locally televised show, Bernie Norman had cried, afraid of the old clown's garish orange and white face, the red lips, the yeasty breath that reminded him of his old man. Bernie's dad never failed to bring up this episode, usually on Christmas Eve after a few whiskeys. Once he even told the story in front of Hap, who came to eat Christmas dinner with Bernie, his sister Angie, and their parents.

"Only kid I know afraid of Uncle Jingaling," Bernie's father used to say, sitting at the head of the table nearest the ham so he could be sure he got more of it than anyone else, including guests. Then he'd whistle long and slow, shaking his head, as if this failure on Bernie's part determined the opinion his father would hold of his son for the rest of his life.

"Shouldn't've eaten so much ham," Bernie said.

THROWING TARTS AT THE KING AND OTHER STORIES

"Whoa dude. Are you talking to yourself?" A teenager.

Flustered, Bernie located the right key and unlocked the door. As quietly and reverently as if they were entering a church, the class followed their teacher into the Nocturnal House. Inside all eyes strained to see, but only meager, fuzzy light filtered from somewhere behind the glass where the Komodo dragon lurked. Other than what looked like a rock, no one could see a thing, not even each other's faces.

"Oh gosh, could someone help me find the lights?" It must have been the teacher speaking, and Bernie assumed she was addressing him. He moved to the other side of the exhibit room and groped along the wall where he thought he'd find lights before he remembered. Surely the teacher knew this. He cleared his throat.

"This is the Nocturnal House," he began. "They, uh, regulate the lighting for the Komodo dragon's habitat from inside his cage, if you will," (he knew it wasn't called a cage but he didn't know what exactly to call the glass encased home, and why was he suddenly speaking like this? *If you will*???) "and of course I don't have a key for any exhibits..."

The teenagers snickered. Adults and kids sighed and made irritated sounds. One mother complained, "What's the point of going to see the Komodo dragon if you can't see the Komodo dragon?" Another said, "Some Reptile Roundup."

A voice piped, "Dad, you said we'd see the Reptile House at night."

Bernie imagined the teacher's consternation. The Zoo hosted these educational programs for its members. They were supposed to be fun, too.

"....but I have a flashlight," Bernie continued.

The group quieted and looked around to locate Bernie's voice where he stood at the back of the room.

"The rocks in the Komodo dragon's habitat are temperature regulated, and he likes to sleep on them," Bernie said. He pointed his unlit flashlight at the glass. "Usually I find him sleeping right there." Bernie turned on the beam. For a moment it was difficult to differentiate the Komodo dragon from the craggy rock on which he dozed. Was he even breathing? Then the lizard cracked one eye and lazily regarded his audience so at first it appeared the rock was animate. Children and adults screamed and squealed. The teenagers hooted appreciatively.

As he did every time he saw the dragon, Bernie imagined himself headfirst in its jaws, only his clod-hoppered feet visible and kicking. He shuddered.

His flashlight enabled him to see that the teacher looked somewhat relieved.

"Is there just one?" a child asked, addressing Bernie and not the teacher now.

"Just one. Name's Kyle. He has no mate but they are going to find him one, right?" Bernie deferred to the teacher.

"Right. They're shipping her next month. Her name is Kate."

Kyle and Kate. Kate and Kyle. Bernie had read about the carnivorous ways of the Komodo dragon. As he walked outside and waited for the Reptile Roundup class to leave, he wondered if they would try to eat each other, the way the female praying mantis eats the male after they mated. He sniffed the air. The cool evening breeze brought honeysuckle, and seemed to quell the more rancid odors. The Nocturnal House doors swung open and the class filed out, tittering and laughing as they walked the blacktopped paths of the zoo, still warm and elastic as chewing gum from the day's heat. As he locked the door, Bernie felt a hand on his wrist.

"Thank you." It was the teacher. "You *saved* my ass."

"My pleasure." Bernie blushed, grateful for the semi-darkness.

"I'm Susan Murphy," she said.

"Bernie Norman." They began to walk toward the Owl Education Center near the Zoo entrance. "I guess you can't blame them for getting mad. They think, "Reptile Roundup," they want to see some reptiles."

"I show them a milk snake, a baby crocodile, and a turtle in the classroom, but yeah, you're right."

"What's the deal with the...curator, anyway?"

"Dr. Cook? Oh, the Reptile House is his life. The exhibits—they're like his children. I can't blame him. He's super-protective and won't let anyone have access after hours."

Bernie said, "Me, I've got the key. I have to do a security check at 10 pm every shift, so I am an exception to the rule."

"Really." Susan stopped and looked at him, a thoughtful expression flitting across her face briefly. They walked on to the Owl Education Center.

"Maybe you and I could go sometime." Bernie stopped. What was he saying? His heart pounded in his throat. "You could tell me more about the anacondas. I'm very interested in reptiles. I had a pet iguana once, but it died." He breathed heavily, sucking up air. Why couldn't he shut up?

"Aw." Susan looked down at her shoes. Then she looked up, and said brightly, "Well all right. Thanks again. Here's where I get off." She smiled. "See you around."

"See ya." Bernie wondered, looking with some guilt at the ass with pizzazz, reflecting how that sort of rhymed. The ass he *saved*. He wondered if she was just talking or if she meant she would go with him to the Reptile House sometime. If she was serious, he must be prepared.

Saturday morning Bernie wore his City of Spruce Grove Refuse softball team shorts, new gym shoes, and a plain red t-shirt to the Spruce Grove Rec Center. Hap, who accompanied him despite Bernie's reluctance, had dressed with care for the occasion. Wearing his own new pair of trainers, some new gym shorts and a shirt designed to wick away moisture from sweating during workouts. He even had a set of gloves for weightlifting. After buying his membership and bringing Hap in as a guest (Hap was going to think about joining) Bernie started jogging slowly on a treadmill to warm up.

"Forty-five minutes of cardio a day, weights a few times a week, a few less sandwiches, I'll get in shape,"

Bernie thought. He glanced at Hap, who was nearby watching a woman, probably about forty. Her hair was the color and consistency of cornsilk; her behind was two small, firm grapefruits in her leggings. She turned around and Bernie thought that her face looked a little leathery from too much sun, but her breasts, even though flattened somewhat by black Lycra, were two steep ski slopes. Hap's mouth dropped open.

"Hap," Bernie said quietly, "they were kind enough to allow you to come here as my guest and inspect the premises. Please do not get us kicked out for harassing one of these nice ladies."

"Yeah, yeah, sure, sure." The blond lady was now marching on the stair stepper, the grapefruits flexing, a miracle. "I am inspecting the premises."

"Why don't you buy a membership, Hap? We could do this together. I wouldn't be alone in my misery," Bernie huffed, already winded.

"Maybe I will."

"Be good for you." Bernie mopped his brow with a towel as he jogged. His treadmill faced a large pane glass window overlooking the parking lot from the second floor of the rec center. A silver hatchback pulled up and parked. Wearing a pair of black bicycle shorts, an oversized white t-shirt, her hair pulled back into a ponytail, out came none other than Susan Murphy. He knew it was her—he had perfect vision.

"I don't believe this," Bernie whimpered, but Hap wasn't listening. Should he stay or flee? Before he could decide, Susan Murphy entered the workout room behind him and started on another stair stepper next to the blond lady. Bernie watched out of the corner of his eye, horrified, as Hap sauntered up behind the ladies, checking them out.

"Oh my God," he squealed quietly. Hap moseyed around the blond lady's high tech black metal contraption and spoke to her. At first it seemed to Bernie that the blond lady ignored him, but then he saw, Hap was laughing a little and the lady seemed to relax as she climbed to nowhere. From what Bernie could make out, she spoke to Hap in a friendly voice, not a threatened one. She wasn't running away at least. He strained his neck trying to see Susan's expression. She appeared to be smiling at Hap and the blond lady. Okay. No one felt harassed, Bernie was pretty certain. He'd learned early with his old man, knew when to hide under the bed at the first sign of his surly footsteps. Even now he could hear his mother's pleading voice, see his father circling her and his sister at the kitchen table. Like hikers playing dead to avoid mauling by a grizzly bear, they'd all learned to remain expressionless, so he could find nothing to attack in them. Then one day Bernie's dad keeled over from a heart attack at work and never regained consciousness.

"My father, the asshole," Bernie muttered. "He who laughs last, Dad."

"What? Are you talking to me? Oh, hello!" Susan said when she recognized Bernie. She hopped up on the treadmill next to him. Bernie gasped for air.

"Hi!" He craned his neck again to see that Hap's whereabouts were still at the blond lady's side. He and Susan jogged together in silence for awhile.

"You shoulda heard the lines that guy was feeding that lady," Susan said, laughing. "Too funny."

Thinking he might suffer a coronary right there in front of her, mentally kicking himself for all the salami he'd eaten in his 27 years, Bernie could do no more than nod.

"She asked him what he does for a living, and he goes, "Refuse management." She says, "You mean you're a garbage man?" But get this." Susan rolled her eyes. "She says, "You must be very strong." She affected a seductive growl."

"Oh brother."

"They're hitting it off. Takes all kinds, doesn't it?" Bernie heard the surprise in Susan's voice. Maybe it wasn't surprise, maybe it was wonder. "I know it's mean, but he's such a lizard."

"I thought you liked lizards."

"Not when they look human. Anyway, I like crocodilians more."

"Crocodilians? Millions and millions of green crocodilians."

"There's an albino one at the Reptile House."

"Albino. You mean pink? A pink crocodile?"

Susan burst into laughter. "No, it's white!"

Hap tapped Bernie's shoulder. "I have inspected the premises and hit the jackpot," he said, holding up a slip of paper with the name Roz Parker written on it in blue ink, and a phone number.

"Oh, you know him." Susan sounded suddenly embarrassed. "I didn't…"

Bernie stopped jogging and got off the treadmill. Time to go.

Hap said, "Bernie's my vice president in charge of recycling."

"Is he serious?" Susan asked.

"I'm a garbage man by day," Bernie said. His stomach growled loudly enough for Susan and Hap to hear.

"You two know each other?" Hap now asked, staring at Susan.

"We both work at the Zoo," she said.

From memories of earlier, similar situations with women, where Hap might be present, Bernie thought the way Susan said this conveyed a coolness that he understood meant that they were not friends, just acquaintances. They would never be friends. Would never go to the Reptile House after hours on his watch. What killed him was, none of this would be lost on Hap, either. It was as if Hap had something on Bernie, knew perhaps what his hope had been, and because Hap was his only real friend, it was okay, but it was also not okay, as Hap would ride Bernie about this failure, tease him mercilessly, mess with his brain and come up with schemes that Bernie didn't wish to pursue. Bernie would be left wishing he didn't know, had never known, Hap Weiss, that he could somehow divorce himself from this relationship, both work and personal, forever. But Hap had grown up on the same street as Bernie, walked to school with him, an older protector that Bernie grew to wish he might escape. Hap had helped him get a job. You can't just burn your bridges, even if friendship with Hap had been a little like hopping from one frying pan at home into another fire. Hap had a way of letting Bernie know he knew the worst about him. An angel or a devil? on Bernie's shoulder whispered, *That's what friends are for*, but at times it almost seemed like blackmail to Bernie. At times, it didn't seem friendly, but menacing. Maybe he was just paranoid. Bernie supposed all friendships were this way. Hap knew about his old man, knew Bernie was a softie (on bad days he called him a pussy), that he was shy and ate too much. Well, all anyone has to do is look at me to know that, Bernie thought.

"Bernie helped me out in a very difficult situation this week. He was brilliant. Everyone loved him." Susan smiled at Bernie, who was still mopping his head at the treadmill. She described for Hap what happened that night at the Nocturnal House. Dazed and still sweating, Bernie didn't hear a word. He stood, waiting for the ordeal to be over.

"Are you still going to show me the Reptile House after hours some time?" Susan squatted to tie a shoelace, then stood up.

"Sure."

"How about tonight?"

Hap whistled quietly, folded his slip of paper, and put it in his wallet.

"You didn't tell me you met someone." Hap eyed Bernie in the car as he drove him to his house.

"It's nothing, Hap. She's just a very nice lady." Then he made an old joke, one Hap used to tell Bernie. "Can't I take you anywhere?"

Hap ignored him. "It's nothing. Didn't you hear her? You're going to meet her at the Reptile House, after hours, my friend."

"Sheez. We both work there. I asked her to tell me about the anaconda. She's just being nice. Believe me, Hap. I know this."

"I don't know…"

"Hap, don't get any ideas." Bernie worried Hap might show up at the Zoo, too. This wasn't an impossible feat for Hap, who Bernie knew had broken into small stores and homes in his youth, if not to steal, to do pranks.

Hap was silent a moment. Then he said, "You never let me go."

"What?"

"You never took me. You never even asked."

"To the Reptile House? Are you crazy? You'd get me fired."

"You're gonna take her and not me?"

"She won't raise any suspicions. She *works* there." Bernie pulled up in front of Hap's house. "I love you

Hap, but you know, you can be trouble with a capital T sometimes."

"I resemble that comment. OK. Be that way. See you Monday, if I don't show up to watch you make cha-cha with the Zoo lady."

"Hey hey. Don't talk like that."

Without turning around, Hap waved his arm in the air, to say goodbye, to wave away his words, or both, Bernie didn't know.

On the way to the Zoo that night Bernie felt none of the usual fatigue, just excitement mixed with a sensation of nervous uneasiness in the pit of his stomach, about seeing Susan. Despite what he told Hap, that she was just being nice, Bernie had hopes. To prevent sure disappointment, he repeatedly quashed those hopes as they arose in his mind: a scene in which he saved Susan from a loose Komodo dragon; a scene in which they held hands before the reticulated python's cage. Bernie clapped a sweaty hand over his face, covering it, and rubbed his eyes. This most welcome sign from Susan, that he wasn't a complete loser, was hard to believe, but he would take it. He felt grateful, whatever it meant.

Passing the gorilla habitat, Bernie heard a bellow and decided to go in. Across the gaping cliff between them, one silverback sat chewing grass, one rubbed its back on a rock, and the third lay on the ground on its back, scratching its belly.

"Hey!" Bernie motioned to the gorilla that chewed grass. He danced around, pounded his chest, made a few boxing jabs in the air, accentuating each punch with "Tora, Tora, Tora," a movie his father once forced him to watch. The gorilla that had been lolling on the ground got up, turned her back to Bernie, and pissed a pungent stream. Bernie smoothed his uniform and laughed a little nervously.

He was to meet Susan at 9:45 in front of the Reptile House. At 9:30 a jazz trio packed up their instruments and left the amphitheater. Bernie strolled through the zoo as nonchalantly as he could pretend toward his destination. Suddenly he realized—Susan wouldn't come. It had all been a prank. He had been crazy to believe her! Again he smacked his forehead with his palm.

"What are you doing?" Susan materialized from behind some Japanese maples. Bernie almost jumped.

"I...I'm getting bit up by these mosquitos." He pretended to swat at bugs.

"They leave me alone," Susan said seriously. "It must have something to do with your blood, or your scent. Or maybe they just like you." She smiled.

Sweat poured in droplets from his forehead. His hair felt damp. Before he could stop himself, Bernie said, "I'm always worried I'll swallow one."

"I know. I've done that before. Yuck." She looked up at him. She was a few inches shorter than Bernie. He stared helplessly down at her, hands at his sides in a gunfighter's stance. The broad surface of Susan's face looked somewhere in between pretty and plain, he decided, smitten. Her complexion and expression were pleasant and clear, her brown eyes, expectant.

"Well, are you going to unlock the door before someone sees us?"

"Yeah." Bernie fumbled with his keys, unlocked the door, and they slipped in. The air inside the Reptile House had a faint fishy odor that always made Bernie imagine a rusty, dripping faucet or a pipe somewhere, leaking sewage.

"I know where the lights are in here," Susan said. She flicked a switch, and Bernie saw that she wore a blue and white striped t-shirt, white cutoff shorts, and white sandals. Her legs were smooth and brown. Overwhelmed, he resisted the urge to breathe in the air around Susan's ponytail, and kept his eyes instead on the glass-enclosed exhibits around the octangular room.

"Tell me about the anaconda," he said nervously.

"It's over here."

Their footsteps on the gritty concrete floor echoed in the cavernous domed building. Susan found the anaconda's cage. Its head was hidden, but the rest of its green cable-like body, entwined around the wood of a jungle shrub planted in the exhibit, was clearly visible and looked moist.

"The anaconda is the largest snake in the world and can weigh up to 400 pounds, as heavy as three adults. It can squeeze the life out of a goat or wild pig in less than a minute."

"Have you ever held it?"

"Yes. I mean, I was sitting down…"

"What was it like?" Were you scared?"

"A little, but we're supervised, and once you get the hang of it, it's no big deal. Although there have been attacks on humans, you're more likely to get hit by lightning than strangled by an anaconda or python."

"Huh. I don't know if I would ever get used to it," Bernie said, shaking his head. "You want to do this the rest of your life? This is your career?"

"I don't know. Yes. It depends on how I do in my studies and practicum."

The realization that Susan was seriously jeopardizing her job by being here with him woke Bernie, and he began to worry. "Why are you doing this, Susan?" he asked.

"You mean studying reptiles?"

"No. You could get into trouble."

"You did me a favor. I returned the favor."

"Favor. What favor?"

"Helping me with the Reptile Roundup…"

"No, I mean, what is the favor to me?" Bernie asked, perhaps too intensely, for Susan swallowed hard and wouldn't look him in the eyes right away.

"To make you feel better in front of your friend Hap."

"Oh." What did that mean? And why did it hurt, he wondered. Expectations were bad things to have. Susan was just being nice, but he had hoped. Now, a little resentful, on the defensive to protect a part of the world he knew and understood even though sometimes he hated it, Bernie said, "Hap's not so bad. I've known him since we were kids. He's had a hard life. I guess he kinda grows on you after awhile."

"Like a fungus?" Susan laughed, punching his arm.

"If he's a bit of an asshole, he's reliably so. He doesn't pretend to be nice. I know where I stand with him, you know?" He supposed he wanted her to catch the sarcasm in his voice. Wanted to show her he wasn't stupid, and she noticed all right. Bernie was immediately sorry.

Susan crossed her arms over her chest. "Oh, and I suppose it's not the same with me. I'm phony." Her voice, though suddenly monotone, sounded sharp, harsh.

"You work with reptiles, you don't like lizards, at least human lizards. I wonder what kind of reptile you think I look like. You tell me. Whatever."

"Hey!" she snapped. "Oh, aren't you quite the gentle giant, Gentle Ben, getting all surly on me. Works with garbage, but is ashamed of working with garbage."

She walked a few steps away from him, shook her head, and walked back. She touched his arm and stared at him, forcing him to look at her. Bernie's discomfort, both at being so revealed and so physically close to Susan at the same time, registered in his heated cheeks, which rose up, flushed, under his eyes like two balloons. Gentle Ben? He was a bear now? He pictured himself tipping over garbage cans at Yellowstone and chuckled.

"What's so funny?" she asked.

"Jeez, don't have a cow," he mumbled.

"If you want to know the real truth, Bernard, I have another reason for coming," Susan said. Almost hissing.

Bernie remained silent, waiting. Bernard, that was like his mother scolding him. He didn't want to say anything else wrong.

"A few months ago, Dr. Cook, the guy who runs this place?"

"Yeah."

"He criticized how I handled a timber rattlesnake, and he reprimanded me in front of my fellow students. I had to repeat part of the curriculum before I could teach these classes and get paid as staff. Oh, he's a winner. So, I guess I like having it over on him, you know? That I've been in here when he thinks it's locked and that he's in control. My revenge. Does this make sense? It doesn't have anything to do with you, or not everything to do with you at least."

Was that a compliment or an insult? "Huh. You just like knowing he doesn't know?"

"Exactly. He's not going to find out unless you tell him. I guess you think I'm reckless." She giggled.

"I'm not going to tell him."

"Don't you ever like to have a little fun, a little adventure out of the ordinary? A partner in crime besides

Hap?" Susan's eyes looked wild now, and her pony-tail swung as she punctuated her words. Bernie looked down and said, "But what if the rattlesnake bit you? Maybe Dr. Cook was concerned about that possibility."

"I'm not a child." She turned away again. "But would you care? The rattlesnake is poised, ready to strike. Bernie the security guard just happens to be making his rounds and saves me by slaying the serpent with his bare hands." She laughed, turning to look at him for his reaction. "Well, you did save me once before," she added, a droll smile playing on her lips.

Had she read his mind? Was she teasing him? Who was this woman? Bernie felt steady for the first time that night. He played it as safely as he could. "Yes, I would care," he admitted. "But I don't know about you, you're a little crazy. Anyway this is two favors I've done you, and you've only done one for me. By the way, you didn't have to make me look good in front of Hap. I already look good in front of Hap. Pity is no favor."

"But wait, you idiot." Her eyes softened. "Is that what you thought? Do you think I'm dumb enough to operate out of anything less than pure selfishness? Out of clear Darwinian survival of the fittest? Hey, do you want to see the albino crocodile?"

And later, Bernie was surprised at how natural it seemed when Susan touched both of his cheeks and said, "Ssh. Let's evolve."

Monday morning found Bernie sweeping the street behind the garbage truck again. Hap whistled cheerfully. He'd met Roz Parker at a sports bar to watch the ballgame Sunday, and "things looked promising," Hap said. He waited for Bernie to give him the details about Susan, but Bernie only smiled.

"I don't care. Keep it to yourself. You won't hear me begging you for information. Seems only fair I tell you, you oughta return the gesture," Hap muttered.

By 9:30 a.m. Hap had taken off his shirt and Bernie sported large perspiration stains around his armpits. Already the pavement shimmered. A little girl sat on a curb and offered them ice water in paper cups. As Bernie leaned against the truck to drink and Hap walked around the other side to smoke, Bernie noticed that the little girl kept looking up at a telephone wire, then down at the curb. He watched her through the shimmering haze in a state of overheated fatigue, then curious, followed the girl's gaze up to the telephone wire, where a robin perched, then down again to the curb grass, where a baby robin waddled around like a wind-up toy. It didn't look real, it was so cute. The mother robin gazed steadily at the little girl. The child, as cute as the baby robin in her red polka dot sundress, stared solemnly back.

Bernie chuckled and pushed himself off the side of the truck. Hap slammed the driver's door and started the engine. As Bernie hoisted himself onto the sideboard, he saw that the baby bird had ventured into the street in front of the truck. The little girl looked up at the sound of the engine, then down at the street again as the truck travelled its first few feet and the baby robin disappeared beneath it. The mother robin remained motionless at her perch on the telephone wire. Bernie banged on the side of the truck with his fist. Hap stopped. Bernie jumped down and walked around to the back of the truck where Hap could see him in his mirror.

"What?" Hap shouted irritably.

"Stop! Just, Stop!"

Bernie got the broom and dustpan from the back and walked to the right front wheel of the garbage truck. He looked up at the mother robin, who stared back, her sharp black eyes like beads, expressionless, fathomless. Bernie imagined this was bird body language for shock. He looked at the little girl, her eyes brimming with tears. Hap came over to see what was going on. Bernie bent down to look at the street under the truck, found nothing, then examined the right front tire for a baby robin squashed into a pancake on its treads.

"What happened? Did I run over her doll?"

"It's not your fault, Hap. I didn't get a chance to tell you because it happened so fast...."

A loud cheep sounded from under the truck, and like a feathery rubber ball on springs, the baby robin bounced out. The little girl squealed and shooed the baby robin to safety on the sidewalk.

Bernie mopped his brow and turned to Hap "...the bird. I thought you ran over a baby bird."

"Oh," Hap said. He looked at the little girl. "I guess I better pay more attention. Stick of gum, sugar plum?" He pulled a pack of Animal Stripe Fruit Flavored Chewing Gum from his shirt pocket and offered her a stick.

Bernie threw his broom and dustpan in back and climbed on the sideboard. Hap hit the gas, and the garbage truck moved down the street to other houses. Sweat dried on Bernie's face in the faint breeze from the truck's movement through the air. He hadn't lost any weight yet, but he felt lighter, just keeping some things to himself.

LOGGERHEAD

On the morning of their last day at the beach, Tucker followed his daddy and uncle through condominium parking lots where fishermen gutted and scaled their catches, past gray cedar beach houses, and down a pine boardwalk over the dunes to the sand. The two men, skin tanned the reddish-brown color of strong tea, wore bright purple and orange swim trunks. They moved slowly in the late morning heat, but even so, Tucker, white hair buzzed close to his head, had to run to keep up with them. Daddy carried a few folding chairs and pulled a cooler on wheels that he had to lift when they reached the sand. Uncle Jay hauled a blue and white striped canopy and some blankets. When they found their preferred spot, before they even dropped their gear and gasped for breath, Tucker asked, "Will you play with me now, Daddy?"

"Not now, Tucker. I told you. We gotta set up this tent."

Daddy and Uncle Jay spent the next half hour connecting aluminum pipes and erecting the canopy. During this time Tucker asked the same question three more times. When at last they'd secured the canopy against the constant wind, Uncle Jay and Daddy dug small ditches in the sand for their chairs. They spread the blankets. Tucker's uncle opened the cooler to get beers. The two men sat down with profound relief.

"Don't get much better 'n this," Uncle said.

"Come in the water now, Dad!" He had already built a sandcastle—a cone-shaped mound surrounded by a shallow moat.

Daddy moaned a little. "Not now, Tucker."

"But you said…"

"Tucker, what'd I say? I said at eleven you could have Frookie Cookies. It ain't eleven yet. Why don't you find someone to play with?"

Tucker ran away and the two men chortled deep in their throats.

Frothy water rushed up to grab Tucker's toes. He shrieked and ran again, around and around in the sand on this hazy hot day. The sun burning through clouds, through the rarely still air that felt like a blast furnace. Ain't rained but once, and that was at night when Tucker was asleep, Daddy said. You could hardly even tell in the morning.

Tucker slowed down and passed people sitting on blankets and chairs under umbrellas. He passed the sand-coated limbs of children younger and smaller than him that reminded him of sugar doughnuts. Then there were fewer people. Tucker's feet had grown used to being scalded, but now he ran toward the damper sand at the water's edge that felt cool, like cookie dough. He hesitated, then went a few steps further into the trail ends of waves lapping the beach and screamed again, the water was so cold. But then it felt good. He splashed along the shore and looked back toward their canopy. He could see the blue and white striped tent far away, and waved.

Eleven o'clock came and went and Tucker forgot he was to have cookies. He thought of his mother and aunt out shopping at the stores. They never went in the water, anyway. Sometimes Daddy fished. Everyday Tucker asked them to play with him, but after the first few days they waved him away and made him wait longer, and a little longer. Suddenly somehow the day was always over, everyone packing up, the canopy coming down, and Daddy and Uncle Jay had left what looked to Tucker like a treasure nest of silver eggs, but which were actually about twelve crushed beer cans piled in the sand.

"You just found you Blackbeard's Treasure," Uncle would say every time, handing Tucker a plastic bag. Uncle and Daddy let Tucker put the cans in the bag and carry it to the recycling bin at the cabana.

Thirsty, Tucker slowed to a trot and plopped down at the edge of the waves. A few surfers, slick and black beyond the sandbar, bobbed on their boards. Tucker swallowed. Something stank. Like the garbage dumpster full of fish heads out in the parking lot, but worse. Tucker turned and looked up the beach. A big rock rested against the dunes. He looked back again at the dots of rainbow-colored umbrellas and imagined Daddy standing with a hand on his sunburnt forehead to shield his eyes, looking for him.

The closer Tucker came to the rock, the stronger the smell grew. He would climb it, jump from rock to sand, and climb the dunes. He might hide in the tall grass, make them find him. By the time Tucker neared the rock the smell had become so strong he held his nose and stopped running. He narrowed his eyes to squint. The rock now appeared to be something else, and more colors than just black. Parts of it looked green, some parts orange. Some parts torn away. A turtle! A big, dead turtle! Its head, or a stiff leg, half chewed off.

"Pee-yew!" Tucker shouted. He circled the turtle once. Then, dunes forgotten, he ran back toward Daddy and Uncle.

They were still sitting in their chairs.

"Dad!" Tucker dropped to his knees on a blanket.

"Tucker, where you been?"

"Dad! I saw a big, dead turtle!"

Tucker's Dad rooted in the cooler. He tossed Tucker his cookies and a carton of juice.

"You gotta come see!"

"Aw, Tucker," Daddy scowled.

"It smelled real bad," Tucker begged.

Daddy crushed his beer can and handed his binoculars to Uncle Jay. He slowly rose to his feet but remained a little bent at the waist.

"Hold down the fort," he told Uncle. "How far is it, Tucker?"

"Not far. I get there fast."

"Point to it."

Tucker pointed to a black dot in the sand far up the beach. "There."

Daddy put his right arm on his lower back, bent backwards, and rubbed. He straightened up. "I don't see nothin'."

"There, there!" Tucker insisted. Daddy grabbed the binoculars from Uncle Jay and looked through them. "I don't see anything." He sat back down with a sigh.

"It was alive," Tucker said softly. A seagull screamed and crash-landed on the sand nearby, glassy eyes riveted to his cookies.

"Aw, Tucker. Now you're lyin'."

"I am not, it was alive!" Tucker began to run away again, back toward the turtle, waving his arm for his father to join him. He looked back once. "Come on!"

Tucker knew he was close when he smelled the turtle again. Still, dizzy from heat, from the ocean's movement toward and away from him that made him feel like he was running in place, he wondered what it would be like to float out with the rush of tide that came in faster and more furiously, forcing him to run closer and closer to the dunes. He stopped and shuddered, looking up at the bleached mounds of sand, tall yellow-green grasses swaying against the now clear blue sky. He listened to the surf tumbling shells like pieces of glass or tiny bells, and felt so suddenly sleepy he almost fell down. But then something caught his eye. Was it wind kicking up sand near the turtle? Gulls hovering close above the carcass careened like a pretty white mobile, crying. Tucker ran closer. What looked like seashells or wet rocks moving were the glistening shells of three newly hatched baby turtles digging

ANNE BIANCO

their way out from under the turtle. Sand coated their
sticky claws as they crawled, making slow, deliber-
ate strides toward the sea. Two gulls swooped down,
claiming the same turtle by different limbs, and tore it
in two. Tucker howled and rushed at the birds, but not
before another gull soared off, a second turtle briefly
silhouetted against the sky, dangling from its beak.

One remained. Tucker hovered over the baby turtle and shooed away the relentless gulls by waving his
arms as they screeched and laughed. The last baby log-
gerhead turtle finally reached damp sand, hesitating
just beyond the surf's grasp, when Tucker saw Daddy
trudging toward them.

"Hurry, hurry!" Tucker cried, hopping up and
down like he sometimes did when he needed to pee
real bad.

A wave washed up, flipped the turtle, and rolled it
over a few times before sucking it into the first shallow swell of ocean, where it disappeared.

"That sure is a big, dead turtle, Tucker."

Tucker, throat parched, croaked, "It was alive
once, right Daddy?"

"I guess. Don't smell like it ever was."

DOT

They named her Dot, short for Dorothy. Her black, close-set almond eyes were set in a porcelain complexion and topped with a shock of black hair her mother kept short. She was spare as a fence post, with limbs that shot up lean and pale when she was a teenager.

Dot grew up with her parents and brother Bill in a ranch house on State Route 95 in Bellville, Ohio. She never knew a lack of food or clean clothes. The thought of expecting or wanting more than she was given never occurred to her, and she inherited her parents' love of the orderly and precise.

Dot spoke with a slight lisp and had a habit of biting her tongue and letting her mouth fall open as she labored, concentrating, at some task. She quickly learned jobs more often relegated to her father and brother—mowing, fixing, and building using drywall, mortar, tiles, brick—you name it, Dot could do it—as well as the household chores—cooking, cleaning, and sewing, although no one ever mentioned or praised her for the ability to bridge the gap between these kinds of tasks.

Later in life Dot couldn't remember much about her brother Bill, three years her senior. She supposed they had some good times at Christmas. He moved out and went to work in a machine tool shop while Dot was still in high school, and they rarely saw each other after that but for holidays. Dot never considered herself lonely, though. She knew how to occupy herself.

It wasn't until she was grieving the death of her second husband that Dot felt susceptible to all sorts of intrusions into her analytical, orderly thoughts. Flashes of memories began to poke through her sadness. When she found herself beginning to recall these things, Dot shook her head as she used to shake her Etch a Sketch to erase her mind of the mental pictures, but they persisted and won out.

Her father had spoken very little, and when he did, he'd condensed what he was going to say down into the fewest words. His logic made sense—he spoke this way in order to expend the least amount of energy, to be exact in his meaning, and avoid making too much noise.

When she was six years old Dot came in from playing out in the snow to find her mother standing at the stove, and without looking, adding spoonful after spoonful of sugar to her coffee, stirring and scraping the sides of her ceramic mug. The sound began to irritate Dot, but her mother kept on lifting her spoon, its freight from the sugar bowl as white as the snow outside, dumping the grains into her mug, stirring and repeating the process. She only ever allowed Dot and Bill one spoonful of sugar on their cereal in the morning, although sometimes Billy stole more when she wasn't looking. One day Dot witnessed her mother smiling clear as day, watching Billy put five or six spoons of sugar in his bowl without once correcting him. Now, something about the way her mother stood and stared at nothing seemed very odd to Dot, and she felt a new feeling that she experienced as a quickening of her pulse and an uneasy warmth in her chest and the back of her neck. Her mother rarely stood so still, at least, never for long. She was always busy tidying things her children had messed up. Putting things in order.

Dot removed her mittens, scarf and boots, being sure to keep the wet galoshes on the mat set inside the door just for that purpose as she'd been told, and not to get melting snow on the spotless kitchen floor. The stirring stopped. Dot's mother turned and looked Dot straight in the eye.

"Whatever you do, don't have children," she said.

This led to further memories of times when her mother's expression grew vacant or vague and she appeared to speak to someone or something Dot couldn't see or wasn't actually present in the room. When she was very little, Dot thought her mother was talking to *her*. As she grew older, she realized that wasn't so. Her mother didn't do this when her father was around, and it never occurred to Dot to wonder why or to tell him. In fact, she never once in her lifetime spoke to her mother or anyone else about it.

The other time from her childhood that stood out in Dot's memory was when she was nine and went to the county fair with Mrs. Miller and some girls she knew from the 4H club. Dot had heard about the rides at the fair that were lit up with colored lights at night, and she couldn't wait to go. She'd never felt so excited. She put the folded dollar entrance fee (from money she'd earned shoveling snow) in the pocket of her jean's shorts and ran outside when Mrs. Miller honked her horn in the driveway.

Dot waited in line to present her dollar to the ticket man at the entrance to the fair, and then everyone waded into a lot of noise and commotion. Pie and hot dog eating contests; farm animals you smelled first and saw later; cotton candy and snow cones for sale. Dot couldn't think of anything except the far off sound of a carrousel, and a ride Janie said was called The Mouse Trap, a miniature sort of roller coaster. Dot wanted desperately to go on The Mouse Trap and ride the merry go round. She could feel her mouth spreading into a grin, pushing the flesh of her cheeks up against her eyes.

Mrs. Miller gathered the girls around her once they'd passed through the front gate.

"Stick together and don't talk to strangers. Meet me right here at 4 o'clock. You'll need to buy tickets for the rides over there at that booth." She pointed to a small kiosk just to the left of the entrance.

Dot wasn't sure she'd heard right. Tickets? Hadn't they just paid for a ticket? She didn't want to ask Mrs. Miller in front of the other girls, and she didn't want to go with them only to be unable to ride the rides. Dot had never been to a fair before. Aside from the snacks, she'd merely assumed no additional costs outside the entrance fee. Her parents didn't offer her any spending money, and Dot didn't expect them to—but had they known? Why hadn't they told her?

The other girls rushed to the ticket kiosk, barely noticing that Dot hung back. The last thing she wanted was to be forced to confide in Mrs. Miller or ask her for anything. This was an unspoken rule of her childhood.

"I...I don't have more money for the rides," she finally blurted out. Dot was so mortified, so ashamed. She could almost see the pinkness of heat she felt moving from her neck to sear the flesh of her pale cheeks. She thought she might cry, which she never did.

"I thought I just paid for a ticket and…"

Mrs. Miller clucked her tongue. "You thought that paid for everything? Aw. Well, I don't have much money to give you, otherwise I would. You can stay with me, and we can walk around and see the sights until it's time to go."

Dot felt so grateful that Mrs. Miller hadn't told the others; hadn't humiliated her in front of them or made her feel worse, that she couldn't speak and merely toed the dirt at her feet with her right sneaker.

Mrs. Miller rooted around in her purse. "Hey, don't look so sad, Dot. I've got enough to buy you an ice cream, okay?"

"Oh, no, that's okay. I'm not hungry."

"But Dot, I want to. It's my treat. Would I offer if I didn't mean it?" Mrs. Miller shook her head. "I'll tell the girls you felt sick. Did your parents know you were going today?"

"I don't know, I guess."

It sure hadn't taken much time for that day to go sour. For a long time after, Dot considered the fact that she didn't get to ride The Mouse Trap one of the larger disappointments in her life. She heard later that the ride had broken down with people in the cars. They had to climb off the ride through the tracks, high over the ground, which Dot would have enjoyed.

Dot learned from the experience. It taught her to watch people and events outside of herself until she thought she understood things well enough to avoid similar situations in the future.

In high school Dot conducted research on the most quality education she could get for her money, "the most bang for the buck," as her dad would say. She took college entrance exams and scored well enough in science and math to gain entrance into the computer programming department at a university one hundred miles away from Bellville. When she read her acceptance letter Dot almost shouted, "Hallelujah," out loud. She even received some grants and made up the balance with a loan. If her parents were aware of Dot's efforts and actions, they made no mention. The August after graduation she packed her bags and drove to college in a used but nearly pristine rust-colored Toyota Corolla she'd bought with money from her part-time and summer jobs. She'd negotiated hard with the man behind the desk even when his shoulders rose to his ears, and he snarled, "Blue book price? Blue book?" as if he might suffer a stroke from disbelief that such a book existed.

"Yes, I want to pay the blue book price," Dot had said, all monotone and poker-faced.

Although it was a foreign car, Dot's dad did say, "You got a deal." That was about as far as praise went with him.

"I'll be back at Thanksgiving," she called out the window as she drove away. Her parents didn't wave.

After college a software programming company quickly hired Dot, and she met the man she later married there. They decided to elope in order to avoid dealing with their families, and spent a month travelling in Europe before returning to their jobs.

Dot found the whole idea of eloping romantic. She was crazy about this man. He was good looking with a toned body, smart, a great cook, and funny.

She bought lacy black lingerie and walked around in front of him as he lay in bed. She did whatever he wanted to do. The whole arrangement was idyllic. She'd paid for a new car already, and they were close to paying for their house because they'd lived together for two years before they got hitched. No children, no big bills. Just work, sex, food, and some alcohol on the weekends.

Dot travelled the world in her position as a programmer, spending months in the Netherlands, Germany, and Japan. One day she came home to find her husband a little drunk and resentful.

"You're gone all the time," he said.

"Well, what do you want me to do? It's my job."

Later they had sex, but she was tired, and he was so alternately clingy and sulky that afterwards she got up, took a shower, and fell gratefully into blissful sleep in the guest bedroom.

A year later they began divorce proceedings after Dot discovered he'd begun an online relationship with a French woman who had two children from her current marriage.

He moved to San Francisco to live with her, the French woman. The Frog. That's what Dot's dad called French people.

Dot lost 25 pounds; she called it the Divorce Diet. She never missed a day of work unless she had the flu, which, she never did.

When she went home at the holidays, she kept things brief, fearing her mother's judgement as a failure in her marriage.

"I expect he wanted someone to stay home and cook his dinner," her mother said. "I told you all this education and work would lead to no good. A man needs a woman to take care of him, and all you could do was think of yourself. Always did."

Dot thought she was going to die. She was only 42. After a few years she tried to date. She did it all—online, speed-dating, Christian. She joined clubs to meet people. She joined a church and went on weekend outings with members of the congregation. She went to Newfoundland and paddled a kayak to Quirpon Island. She camped alone. She didn't need anyone to take care of her, but she was lonely.

In this line, one day she decided to take a class in auto mechanics. She was sick and tired of paying someone to do God knows what with her car when it broke, without understanding the problem herself, and understanding what it should cost. "I'll do my own maintenance," she thought. The class met at a vocational school.

The teacher struck her as smiling all the time. He was slightly overweight in a way that wasn't unattractive. He had receding hair, a ruddy face, and blue eyes that laughed. Yes, he was always ready to laugh. He was easy with students of all ages. He didn't condescend. He was fair. Dot realized after two classes that she was attracted to him, not so much for his looks but for how he stood out. He was happy, and it emanated from him and seemed contagious. She began to smile back at him, make repartee at his jokes. Dot, thin as a rail, could have been a young boy with her short black hair. She wore no jewelry, no perfumes. She did still wear her lacy underwear, though. The teacher began to realize that Dot was flirting with him. He asked her out. They fell in love. They married and spent the next five years going to ride their four wheelers and motorcycles on some land Dot bought in Kentucky. They camped out and planned to build a home there.

One day Dot received a call at work. Ben was in the ICU. He'd told her about his congenital heart defect when they first met, but she'd put those things out of her mind. She wasn't one to worry. But Ben died in the ICU a day later. Dot was alone again. The thought of going home to her parents, or even calling them to tell them the news, was insufferable. She wouldn't. They didn't even know about Ben, anyway, and if they had, they would have disapproved. A divorcee carrying on. How could one explain these things about her parents to people living in the 21st century?

Ben's mother had told Dot she could have the burial plot adjoining his. Dot believed Ben's children from his first marriage welcomed and accepted her into their lives, but this was where the rubber met the road. When Ben's mother died, so did the burial plot agreement. Dot had thought grief was what she felt after her divorce. This was an altogether different beast.

And that wasn't the end of it. No. Things got even worse.

Not long after Ben died, Dot's mother called. Dot's father had suffered a heart attack, and his care required more work than she could do, having her own health issues. She asked Dot to help her. After all, it was a daughter's duty to help her mother, right?

Dot wasn't convinced.

"Where's Billy?" she asked. She knew they'd been giving him money for years. She'd seen none of it herself, not even ten bucks for books while she was away at college. They probably figured she didn't need it, and she didn't, although it would have been nice.

"He can't help us. You know he's been disabled for 7 years. He can't work due to his back."

"Well, he's close by," Dot answered. "I live 70 miles away and I'm working a difficult job, Mom. I could come once in awhile on a weekend. I mean, Billy could run errands for you, put in a load of wash, you know..."

"You have always been an ungrateful girl," her mother said. "You were…"

"Mom," Dot began, but she couldn't find the words to say. Dot couldn't find the words because she didn't know what she wanted to say, and anyway, she suspected her mother was right somehow.

"...always selfish and uppity," her mother went on.

Dot hung up the phone.

The following weekend she drove up to Bellville.

Her mother died first, and because her father was now an invalid, Dot placed him in an assisted living facility near where she lived so she could check on him easily. When he died, it was left to Dot to take care of the house and property in Bellville. By this time Billy also resided in an assisted living facility.

In the end, she found out a lot of things she already suspected.

Dot had never known anything about her parents' finances, but now she learned her father had made some unwise investments back in the 90's and lost a great deal of money. She also learned they'd given Billy at least $250,000 over the past 20 years. Dot stopped payment of the dwindling funds still going to her brother and informed him that the stream of income was near depletion, so he would need to dip into his retirement or pension or whatever from the machine tool shop. He wasn't happy to hear this news but was in little position to do anything about it. She told him she'd send half of the proceeds from the sale of the house and property.

Dot went to the house in Bellville on weekends to clear it out, sell what was salvageable, and give away or throw out the rest. It took a year of weekends. Then there was the shed or garage where her father had stored his tools—Dot kept some of these and donated the rest.

Two months after she finished her work, the sheriff from Bellville called her.

"Are you the owner of the house at Poorman and State Route 95?"

"Yes."

"I'm sorry to have to tell you this, ma'am, but your house burned down last night," he said. "Can you come up and take a look at the property and police report, or can I fax it to you?"

"Fax it," Dot said.

Six months later Dot got another call from the sheriff up in Bellville.

"I hate to make a nuisance of myself, ma'am, but I have another problem to report about your property here."

"Shoot," Dot said.

"It appears that late last night, or actually early this morning, a motorist speeding on State Route 95 past your house, I mean, what's left...your property, lost control of his car and drove onto the grass, on through the shed, pretty much destroying it completely. It... the shed...collapsed."

"Are you married?" Dot asked. The sheriff laughed.

A month later Dot had the shed razed; there was nothing left on the land to indicate a soul or souls had once lived there. Perhaps no living soul, including herself, had ever lived there. Perhaps her parents were ghosts. Perhaps she, Dot, didn't exist. She took a picture of the lonely scene with her phone.

When Dot received a diagnosis of breast cancer a year later, it seemed a cinch in comparison to the rest of her life. She didn't fall victim to despair, but instead lived through chemo and radiation as if they were routines to which she'd been accustomed for years. She somehow survived without anger or regret, and without once considering herself remarkable or entitled to more than the cards life dealt her.

THE TRUTH IS, YOU'RE CRAZY

No one could deny her. Mrs. Liepschien had dressed for the occasion. That morning before going to work she'd showered and perfumed, and donned her favorite silk pantsuit. Her thin diamond watch was peeking out tastefully from the billowy sleeves. She'd just had a manicure, a subtle taupe color, not loud. She'd touched up her makeup in the restroom on the way out of the office. Her emerald necklace was tucked into her twice unbuttoned cream blouse, ready to drop out as she might lean over a makeup or jewelry counter. So what, she was flat chested. It wasn't like she was giving everyone a show, for Pete's sake. Her hair, buzzed close to her head like a marine's, was black with iron gray patches at her temples and around her ears—her worry spots, she liked to say, if anyone asked, which, they didn't. She might not be a beauty queen, but she was dressed, coiffed, bejeweled, and smelled fabulous, that much was true.

The acres and acres of the mall parking lot were full of cars, almost to those wastelands near the curbs where Mrs. Liepschien always wondered, "Who in hell would ever park there?" A sale, a sale! McAlpin's. Everyone must have had the same idea. She shopped for the best spot close to the middle of the mall first. Lucky her, someone in a silver Volvo wagon pulled out; kids in their car seats, one dozing, one dazed as their mother backed into the lane and smiled at Mrs. Liepschien as if to say, "Go ahead, enjoy the sale. Take my hard won place. I must feed the children." A good mother too, none of that Sbarro or Chick Filet for them.

The children. Mrs. Liepschien had wanted them but now it was too late. The people who moved in across the street had two lovely children, a boy and a girl. They seemed like nice people, but busy. They had their own lives, like Harry's grown kids who came at the holidays. But Harry's grandchildren upset Bentley, their Westie. He snapped when they petted him too roughly or pulled his tail. Mrs. Liepschien hated to yell at or spank Bentley when it was the children's fault, although she knew they didn't understand. But Harry. He didn't mind yelling at Bentley at all.

"Bentley. Bentley, stop. BENTLEY! STOP BENTLEY! Elly, take him out for a walk."

Harry addressed her like a servant most of the time. When his children were around, Mrs. Liepschien obeyed even as Harry's daughter weakly protested. But when they were gone, she ignored him and prayed for the day his heart would fail as she smoked long menthol cigarettes out on the blacktopped driveway with poor Bentley.

She'd get little, the kids would receive most of the estate. Harry had shown her the will before they were married. So what? She could change a will, had access to all the computer files where the documents were stored. She could easily forge signatures and notarize a document. Just see if she wouldn't. Elly had this conversation with herself before. It was like thinking about suicide. You considered the means but weren't really serious about going through with it.

Well, she could still run up the credit cards, Elly thought as she locked the car door and smoothed her clothes. It was just that when you reached a certain age (for her this had been 44) you realized morality is a leisurely thing, a convenience if you were happy. After all the disappointments in her life Elly saw a vision of herself, in a coffin underground, and understood that she should have taken when she could have, had sex when she could have, which wasn't many times, but still, without shame, eaten, drank, loved, loved when she was presented the opportunity.

What was the difference, morality, when you only went around once?

When Mrs. Liepschien married Harry six years ago she had been 43. At that age you take what you can get, and no one else was asking. That's what she told people sometimes, even when they didn't ask. I mean, beggars can't be choosers. Harry had already been through one marriage, two heart attacks, and double bypass surgery. Still, he had his own charms, a business with three locations in the city. Didn't have to dirty his hands anymore, just hire and manage the people who did. Life had been good to Harry—he had prospered. Mrs. Liepschien had done his bookkeeping for three years before he asked her out—she knew.

Anymore it happened every time. At the door to the mall Mrs. Liepschien's eyes filled with tears. Who in the world cared? Someone exited through the door to her right as she fumbled in her purse for a tissue and dabbed at her eyes. Mrs. Liepschien, Elly, dabbed at her brimming eyes with a tissue, then put it in the pocket of her silk blazer that was a color in between purple and blue. Periwinkle they called it. Harry said it was blue, but no. Elly knew it was periwinkle.

Then going through the mall doors, a Friday's restaurant on her right, and a cheap, second rate jeweler she despised on her left, Elly felt better. She was home, the familiar cookie place (later, later), the mall information desk and cash machine. Beyond, McAlpin's loomed, glittering with holiday stars (Halloween had come and gone last week), and Elly could make out the figures of two women at the entrance to the store holding perfume bottles for shoppers to sample.

First, though, a cup of coffee. Elly sat down in one of the uncomfortable chairs with her Hazelnut decaf and placed the paper cup on an unsteady wooden table. She blew on the coffee and sipped. Now to watch all the lovely people she imagined had far better lives than hers. Except perhaps those pathetic walkers, mostly old. In the mall of all places. Even Elly, who loved the mall, to whom the mall was a home away from home, even she would have picked a nature trail, or her own neighborhood rather than the mall. She supposed they had an excuse if it was raining, or too cold outside. Why, she'd tried to walk in her own neighborhood several times. Once when she'd quit smoking (she was smoking again now, but…) when the new girl (why did she call her a girl? She was a grown woman) across the street moved in. She looked like a teenager, jogging, rollerblading, mowing the vast lawn, raking endless leaves in the fall.

"You look like a schoolgirl," Elly had told the woman, whose name was Carla, when they walked together one summer evening, still light outside. Elly told Carla a bit about Harry.

"He's got a lot of health problems. You know that basketball hoop out on our drive? He's supposed to shoot baskets every day for his cardiovascular exercise, but he rarely does it."

"I've seen him out there a few times," Carla said.

"The night we got married, he couldn't even do it," Elly laughed.

"Do...oh." Carla looked down at the pavement. There were no sidewalks in their neighborhood, a fact that bothered Carla because she didn't feel comfortable with her children playing out in the street. Of course they were still too young to do that, but...

Elly continued. "He's gotten me out of a lot of trouble a few times, though, you see, and he kinda lords it over me. I'm indebted to him."

"Oh," Carla said. "Yeah, I guess I know what you mean, lording some failure over you, reminding you?"

"Exactly," Elly answered. She waited for Carla to ask for specifics, to ask her just what kind of trouble she'd been in, but Carla remained silent, smiling as they climbed a hill lined with red maples and large homes, bigger and newer than theirs a few blocks away.

"I'm a shopaholic," Elly said. "See these shoes I'm wearing? I've got one in every color. I've gotten into some real debt on the credit cards. Nothing Harry can't afford. We've been to counseling for it. Harry knew, helped me out once before we were married."

"Aw, gee," Carla said. "That's tough. It's like gambling, or an addiction, right?"

"What Harry doesn't understand is, I'm looking for love, and those clerks, those ladies at the stores give it to me."

"I sort of know what you mean. I jog and exercise. But I still smoke a little even though I know it's bad for me. It's like a true friend I can count on if I can't count on anyone else. Isn't that weird?"

Even though this wasn't exactly what Elly had meant, still she said, "Yeah, I know. I used to smoke. Finally quit. I watched a friend of mine die of cancer, and I just don't want to make anyone have to take care of me." Elly had suddenly wondered, who would take care of me? A stranger? Certainly not Harry. He couldn't take care of himself.

The two women were silent as they turned the corner onto their street and arrived back at Elly's driveway. They could hear Harry inside yelling sharply, "Bentley. Bentley! Get off the couch!"

"Come on in and meet Harry."

"Oh, I don't want to impose. He isn't expecting me."

"You're not imposing. Come see my house Harry's too cheap to let me fix up."

Carla followed Elly up the driveway to the large ranch house. They walked into a small patio hidden from the street by a white trellis enclosure. Elly opened the sliding door to the house and Bentley tried to run out.

"Bentley. BENTLEY!" Harry shouted but remained in his seat on a plush white leather couch. He smiled at Carla and said hello as he fiddled with the TV remote to lower the volume. He'd been watching *Jeopardy*.

"This is Carla Fields from across the street," Elly said. She stood to one side and let Carla step forward, then looked back and forth at them to watch Harry, and Carla's reaction to him.

"Hello. These are some lovely paintings," Carla said of the artwork above Harry's head on the living room wall. "Are they originals?"

"Yes. Do you collect?" Harry asked, perking up. His voice was gravelly, and his eyes glittered like wet stones.

"I wish," Carla said, smiling. "I mean, I wish we could buy some original art. Right now we sink all our money into fixing up that stupid house."

Elly nodded sympathetically. Harry began to tell Carla about each of the paintings until Elly finally said, "Enough about your old paintings. I want to show Carla the house."

"This is a lovely house," Carla said. "I don't think we'll have a house like this until the kids are in college."

Bentley, who'd so far sat quietly behaving in a corner, suddenly barked and ran forward to jump on Carla's thighs and sniff her crotch.

"Bentley, NO!" Harry grabbed a rolled newspaper to threaten the dog, and Bentley ran under a mauve armchair.

Carla blushed but ignored the incident. "The dark wood in our kitchen. Ugh." She scrunched up her nose. "All the tacky wallpaper from the 1970's, the pet-stained carpet…"

"See, we painted our kitchen cabinets, but I still want a new kitchen," Elly said. Behind them Harry snorted and turned up the volume on *Jeopardy* again.

"Well, I do," Elly shouted good-naturedly back at him.

"This isn't bad at all," Carla whispered so as not to bother Harry. "I'd be satisfied with this."

"Well," Elly said, and led Carla through the beige carpeted rooms, stain free, with tasteful furniture choices, hardware, and modern bath fixtures, glass block shower stalls, untouched by dust or fingerprints, all top of the line and contemporary.

"Let my kids come in here for one minute and they'd destroy everything," Carla said, shaking her head.

"Yeah, but they're more important than furniture, or a house," Elly insisted.

"Yes, but I wonder if you'd feel that way if your house never looked this clean and kept up," Carla said. "Think about it."

"That's true. Bentley is enough trouble. I don't mind, but Harry does."

They returned to the living room.

"I'd better go give the kids their bath," Carla sighed. "It was nice meeting you, Harry."

"Nice meeting you." Harry tried to sit up or stand, then settled back into the couch with his remote.

"I'll take Bentley out for a minute," Elly said, hooking a leash to the dog's collar.

They went outside and walked down the driveway.

"When would you like to walk again?" Elly asked.

"The problem is that I'd rather jog, because I get a better workout," Carla began. "If I walk, I'd want to walk 3 or 4 miles at least, and I don't know if you're up for that." She smiled down at Bentley and wouldn't look Elly in the eye.

"I could go as far as I wanted and come back," Elly said.

"My time is so limited, Elly, with the kids, that I have to take it when I can get it, and that's not always on your schedule. You work. It's when I can get away, when Mark gets home from work, you know? I don't think you'll be able to count on me being a regular partner, but we can do it again sometime soon if you like." She didn't mention a time.

"Yes," Elly said, "I'd like."

"Well, see you soon," Carla said, crossing the street. Elly watched her go, trying to imagine what she might do next. Bathe those lovely children, read them stories. She'd seen the lights on in their rooms, heard Carla's voice reading as she stood waiting for Bentley to do his business. Heard the yelling and crying when someone was bad or got hurt. So much life! Once she even heard Carla fighting with her husband. They always seemed to work it out, even if it looked like Carla bore the brunt of all the yardwork. Elly had seen Carla up on the roof cleaning out the gutters! She and Harry had a lawn service, a housecleaner, and a regular handyman.

One summer night Elly waited after dinner for Carla to appear. At 7p.m., Carla strode out the front door in her sweats and gym shoes and started down her front lawn. Elly waved, began to walk down her driveway to cross the street and join her, but Carla veered to the left to pick up a toy from the front lawn and then turned to go back into her house.

Elly finished her coffee and looked at her watch. Six o'clock. She threw her cup in the garbage and walked past a fountain surrounded by ferns. At the entrance to McAlpin's a young woman, tall, her blond hair twisted into a stylish knot, approached Elly with a perfume bottle.

"Would you like to try Siren?" she asked sweetly.

"No thanks, honey," said Mrs. Liepschien. Then, "Why, am I going to set off alarms when I wear it?" Elly wore only Red, perfume, not cologne.

She spent the next hour browsing through the women's designer clothes on the second floor but found nothing that moved her. Later she discovered a

THROWING TARTS AT THE KING AND OTHER STORIES

purse that was marked down. At the cosmetics counter she bought some new mascara, two new lipsticks, and a facial cleanser/moisturizer set. Then, time for fine jewelry. Elly left the cosmetics counter and walked to the nearby jewelry cases. Gina Bevaqua was waiting on another customer, a young thing dressed in jeans and a leather jacket. She had long black hair, and was holding hands with a little boy also dressed in jeans and a denim jacket with cute little cowboy boots. As the young woman peered down into the jewelry case and asked a question, Gina glanced over and noticed Elly. One of her dark pencilled eyebrows rose slightly, then she smiled and concealed a yawn with one of her perfectly manicured hands. Elly put her fist to her mouth as if trying not to giggle, and politely waited her turn while inspecting the diamond rings.

"How much is that one?" the young lady asked.

"Mommy, I want to go now," the little boy whined.

Gina Bevaqua took her time opening the glass door behind the case with a little key as the boy continued to squirm. "This one?" she pointed to a diamond and emerald tennis bracelet.

"No, the one next to it."

Gina located the bracelet and checked a small white tag. "This one is $799," she said in her soft Italian accent. Her brown hair framed cheeks as full and rosy as apples. Gina held the bracelet up to the light, dangling it tantalizingly. She gave the bracelet to the young woman to inspect. "How much did you want to spend?" she asked indifferently, glancing back at Elly.

"I...I wasn't ready to buy anything just yet. I'm still shopping around for the best price," the woman answered. Her gaze lingered on the bracelet in her hand before she returned it to Gina.

"Oh," said Gina, placing the bracelet back in its place, closing and locking the door.

"Hello Elly, and how are you today?" Gina asked, gliding a few paces behind the counter to greet Elly with her warmest smile, her rouged cheeks blossoming further. She was not a tall woman, not really large, but something about Gina's attitude and demeanor suggested to Elly strength, solidness, maybe even force. Elly was overcome with pleasure at Gina's familiar welcome.

"I'm fine, Gina, and how are you?"

"Could be better, but what else is new?" Gina shrugged, frowned, then smiled again.

"I know what you mean," said Elly, and meant it.

"What brings you here today?"

"What else? Twenty five percent off fine jewelry."

"Yes, selected pieces. Did you have something in mind? Last time it was watches, no?"

"Yes," Elly answered, pleased again that Gina remembered these details about her. "But today I want to look at the tennis bracelets. Not for me, for my stepdaughter who's turning 37 next month."

The young black-haired woman in the leather jacket glanced up at Elly, then peered down into the jewelry case again, barely mollifying her child. "If you give me a few more minutes, I'll buy you an Icee, okay?" she told him. The child sat down next to her, kicking at the floor with his cowboy boots. "So, 25 percent off of $799 would be, what?" she asked Gina.

"Are you talking to me?" Gina turned her head toward the young woman. "I didn't know you were still here."

"Yes. I wondered what 25 percent off $799 would be? What would the price be then?"

"Well, figure a quarter of about $800 would be $200, so about $600, before taxes," Gina said. She turned back to Elly.

"That's still a lot," the young woman murmured to herself. "I think I'm out of my league here."

Gina chuckled softly. "It's a good deal," she threw back over her shoulder without turning around. "That's an exquisite piece." Her brows contracted. "Wait a minute. I don't think that one's on sale anyway." Gina put on a pair of large tortoise shell glasses that hung from her neck on a gold chain. She bent to open the case again, and peered at the tag. "No, this one isn't on sale. It's $799. Only those with blue dots on the tag are on sale. So this is still $799," she said looking up at the woman from behind glasses perched on the end of her nose.

The woman's body sagged a little as she leaned over the counter. Elly felt sorry for her.

"Why dontcha get your husband to buy it for you, honey," Elly said.

The young woman turned and glared at Elly, furious. Elly saw that she was beautiful, possibly even younger than she'd guessed. It also vaguely occurred to her that perhaps she wasn't married, didn't have a husband."

"Oh, forget it," the young woman said. "Come on, Sean. Let's get your Icee."

"Well. So. The tennis bracelets. Any stone in mind?"

"Sapphires."

"Over here." Gina opened another case.

Elly finally chose a diamond and sapphire bracelet that cost $759.04, after the sale and a little deal from Gina Bevaqua for being such a good customer.

As Gina packed the boxed bracelet into a McAlpin's bag, Elly asked, "So Gina, can I take you out for a cup of coffee or a drink?"

Gina smiled. "I'm sorry, Elly. I know I promised last time, but this is Moonlight Madness. We're open to midnight tonight, did you know?"

"Oh, that's right. I forgot," Elly said. "I guess I'll just look around then, get this wrapped. Do you go on a break anytime soon?"

"I'm the only one working jewelry tonight, and I don't like to leave," Gina said, gesturing with her arms at the cases. "Some other time, eh?"

"All right. Another time." Elly moved away.

"Bye, Elly. I hope your stepdaughter enjoys the bracelet."

"Yes. Goodbye Gina. But hey," Elly whirled around, her voice rising. "You always say 'another time.' I just want to know when it's going to be *my* time, that's all. I think you make up excuses. Sure, it's fine to be nice to me when I'm spending a lot of money to buy your jewelry, but how come you can't be my friend?"

Gina Bevaqua sighed and leaned on the jewelry counter, elbows on the glass, cheeks resting in her hands. "Elly," she said gently, "I don't like to mix business and pleasure, you know that."

"What's a friendly cup of coffee, a drink, some chat? It's no big deal. It's not like I want you to be my best friend or anything."

Gina stood up and straightened her glasses. She gestured with her hands as she spoke, always an endearing trait to Elly. "All right, you want me to tell you why I don't go with you? Because you kind of crazy, that's why. You start talking about Harry, and, and all those debts....I don't want to be involved. You come in, you gonna buy a little piece of jewelry, it's okay, fine. But I don't want to be involved with your shopping troubles or whatever you call it…"

"Oh, I resent that," Elly hissed, clutching her purse close to her heart. "Shopaholic. I'm a shopaholic."

Gina pointed a finger at her. "That. You crazy sometimes, okay? I gotta watch out for you, Elly. I do it here. I don't let you do over a grand, okay? That's how I am your friend, okay?

"I'm not that bad, Gina," Elly sniffed.

"I know, Elly, but…"

Elly thought about it, staring down at her feet like a child caught in the act of stealing cookies before dinner. She felt shook up, but maybe it was for her own good.

"So you do care for me. That's sweet," Elly said, but her lips curled back as if she tasted something bitter.

"Yes, Elly," Gina said, her eyes full of something— was it concern? pity?—that made Elly cringe. But she smiled.

"Okay, Gina, that's fair enough," Elly said, nodding her head. "I'll buy that." She turned to leave again. "I'll be seein' ya," she called over her shoulder. *Not on your life. I'll show you the power of plastic!*

At first it hurt, but, Elly admitted to herself as she walked out of McAlpin's toward the Blue Chip Cookie Company to appease her loneliness with two or three white chocolate macadamia chip cookies, wasn't it refreshing when someone levelled with her? No one ever told her the truth. Her hair was "interesting" or "stylish" when Elly knew it made her look butch. They told her they'd go for walks and avoided her. They asked her to marry them because they needed someone to do their laundry and take care of them in their old age.

Beggars can't be choosers, Elly thought. There ought to be more people like Gina Bevaqua around.

THE MONROES

In the early 1970s, a priest who used to say Mass at St. Malachi's on Cleveland's near west side inspired his parishioners to get involved with the poor by feeding them at a soup kitchen and helping them get legal aid. My family weren't members of that Catholic parish, but sometimes my mother took us to Mass there. My parents met the Monroes when my mother became involved with this community, back when she was still a Democrat, voted for McGovern, and watched the Watergate hearings while ironing my father's shirts in front of the television in our living room. I went with my mother a few times in winter, taking our largest pots full of mashed potatoes. Looking back, I guess I felt the whole idea was a little crazy (although extremely generous and admirable) for my mother, who had eight children. To feed the poor when we were just barely making ends meet ourselves—our largest pot of mashed potatoes fed my family at one sitting. But I also felt very pious and good for helping the poor, until one time I had to serve them myself, and a man without shoes in winter angrily ordered me to put more mashed potatoes on his plate.

This priest, who I'll call Father B, came to my house once with a very tall black man. Besides once meeting a black man named Britt who painted our house, this was the only other person of color I'd ever met (unless you count watching television, where I saw black people on *Electric Company* and *Sesame Street*). My neighborhood in Lakewood was just a block away from Cleveland proper. The first suburb to the west, Lakewood was a small city in its own right, and totally white when I grew up there. The western suburbs of Cleveland were the still unintegrated parts of town, while the east side, with Cleveland Heights, Shaker Heights, etc, possessed the arts, Jewish people, the residences of high-ranking Cosa Nostra, and black people. I still remember this tall black man who came with Father B telling my little brother, who had been chased home by a bully, "Let's you and me go back up to school and tell him I'm your big brother."

Father B had a pierced ear and looked like a hippie to me because his blond hair was rather long. He'd protested the Vietnam War by breaking into Dow Chemical Company in Washington, DC to raise awareness and oppose their production of napalm, Agent-orange, and body bags. I thought he was the coolest priest I'd ever met. The priests at our parish of St. Clement's in

Lakewood were clean shaven. Tall Father Rogers was friendly and kind of cute with short brown hair and dreamy blue eyes. He reminded me a bit of Dick Van Dyke, and I wondered if at any moment he might start dancing like Burt the chimney sweep in *Mary Poppins*, but the most he ever did was throw pieces of chalk at some of the boys. I think one of the nuns, Sister Rita, fell in love with him, or so I heard.

Father Waldron had flashing black eyes and jet black hair like my father. I felt afraid of him because he swooped across the blacktopped parking lot from the rectory to the sacristy in his black robes like a big bat while we waited for the bell to ring in the school-yard. Often he raised his voice angrily in what I could make out of his sermons, so that, staring at my shoes in feet that reached just past the edge of the pew bench, in a near nap or fidgeting with the missalette, I bolted to attention. Monsignor Seward was old and powdery white as a snowball cookie, but I later heard from my next door neighbor Mrs. Dehaney, after she'd had a few drinks at Christmas time, that he was known to chat up a certain blond at the bar down at The Blue Fox. Of course, I wasn't supposed to have heard this... and anyway in terms of today's scandals, it was noth-ing. In contrast to these priests, though, Father B with the pierced ear, who'd been arrested in what I would later think of as a just cause, and who lived amongst the poor and criminals, like Jesus, was arguably the coolest priest of any my family had ever met.

I'd recently had my own ears pierced. My mother gave me this as a birthday present when I was in third grade. Before the fad hit the newly built malls, and long lines of teen and pre-teen girls waited at jewelry counters in department stores to have the procedure done. She took me to our chain-smoking Dr. Shumacher, (it's possible the man had a butt in the corner of his mouth when he was punching holes in my ears) who broke the first imitation emerald earrings she bought for the occasion when trying to put them on. He cursed under his breath, and had to stitch some thread through the holes in my ear lobes until we returned a week or so later with some amber earrings my mother found to replace them. I gave Father B the remaining unbroken emerald earring to put in his one ear, and I remember how he smiled and thanked me as he drank coffee with my mother and the tall black man at our dining room table.

My parents somehow met Faith and Dick Monroe through Father B and his community on the near west side. One day Faith and Dick came to visit us with their kids. They were Dickie, Jimmy, Marty, and Suzie. My mother put potato chips out in a plastic bowl for the occasion, a very rare treat, and pop. Jimmy came in, plopped down on the couch and said, "Where's the dip?" Marty climbed on the furniture. Dickie stood somewhere shrugging and looking uncomfortable. I don't remember where Suzie was, maybe out on the porch with her parents. I was probably ten or eleven years old; Marty was my age, Jimmy a little older, and Dickie was my oldest brother Joe's age—14 or 15.

My parents sat out on the front porch with Faith and Dick, drinking a few beers. The rest of us sat inside watching an impossibly small (by today's standards) black and white television that we had to smack every once in awhile to get a clear picture. Or jiggle the antennae.

With her mop of short, thin brown hair, her slight figure and her manner of dress, Faith resembled a teenage boy. She had a tendency to slump in her posture, something my mother attributed to bad nutrition from growing up poor. I think my mother immediately liked Faith because she was Polish, like herself, and had also grown up poor (although she never said that, but I *inferred* it). Apparently Faith had some resentments against the Catholic Church (a heresy my mother could overlook in her case) and didn't go to Mass anymore; that is, until my oldest brother Joe died in 1991. As a child she felt she had been mistreated by the nuns in her school because she was poor and sometimes came to class dirty or in old clothes. She wouldn't have been the first kid to be mistreated by nuns. I, having had a much better experience of Catholic school, had a few favorite nuns, and in fact, for awhile I thought I wanted to be a nun! But some with names like Sister St. George and Sister Kevin nearly pulled the cheeks off the faces of mischievous boys.

Faith's wardrobe consisted of jeans or cutoff shorts, sneakers without socks, and oversized sweatshirts. There was no doubt in my mind that she was cool for an adult. She and Father B didn't seem like most adults I knew. Her almond-shaped brown eyes were set in an oval face and always looked surprised. High cheekbones suggested her Slavic background, and the lips of her small mouth stretched thinly over an overbite. Faith often kept her mouth closed over her teeth (as those of us with overbites are wont to do), but like me, when she smiled, man, she was all in. Her teeth hung out big and white and crooked and her smile nearly blinded you with its radiance.

Mr. Monroe, or Dick, on the other hand, was very tall and more serious, although he liked to laugh too. He worked as an electrician, so it seems appropriate that I thought of him as a silver man, silver like wire. He had prematurely gray hair that had probably been blond when he was young, and his perennial tan set it off. It was not the dry white hair of the very old, but strong and sterling. His small blue eyes, rimmed by dark black lashes, stood out sharply in his complexion. A thin mouth occasionally curled into a tight smile. Not only did I think of Dick as a silver man—he actually resembled The Tin Man in *The Wizard of Oz*. I recall him popping his head in the front screen door at one time during this particular visit to check on his sons, and advising Marty in a stern voice not to climb on the furniture. His voice, when he talked, which wasn't often, was mid-range in pitch and seemed to emerge from the corner of his mouth in clipped bursts.

Dickie, their oldest son, was an enigma to me until I grew older and realized he was gay and either autistic or had some affective disorder. Pretty unfortunate combination for a kid in that, or perhaps any, era. He looked a bit freakish, like a child in a man's body, in his early teens. When I later saw the cover of Gunter Grass's *The Tin Drum*, it reminded me of him. He had a broad forehead, a wide-open, innocent face, but like his father's, rather pretty, angelic. Unearthly blue eyes, a thin mouth, rosy cheeked, he didn't say much, but when he did it both sounded, and usually was, very odd in both tone and content. The sound reminded me of the Beatles' helium-influenced voices when they sang "Strawberry Fields," and was often petulant. To give an example, if we were all sitting watching television as we were that particular evening, Dickie might say something completely out of the blue and unrelated to anything that was going on, at which point Jimmy and Marty would shake their heads in disgust, call him a faggot when his parents were out of earshot, or both. Usually they got up and left. Of course, I didn't understand any of this at the time. On my first exposure to the Monroes, I didn't see how different Dickie was from the others. He seemed nice enough to me.

Jimmy, his mother's favorite, was beautiful with the fine features of his father, but his hair was brown. As a teenager he grew it long in the style of the seventies. A trace of a mustache like dirt sat atop his upper lip. His blue eyes appraised any scene from under sleepy lids, and he resembled a rather bored cat who can somehow focus instantly, spring up and pounce on a mouse, and then retire again, sated for the time being. He had a lanky, athletic build, but was not as tall as his father. Before junior high Jimmy was already a lady's man.

While Jimmy was smooth, Marty seemed to be hyperactive, or have ADD, or at least to have some kind of chip on his shoulder about Jimmy. His hair was blond but he was brown-eyed. I may have attributed more intelligence and perception to his deep brown eyes, his mother's, than was ever really there. He too had a long, trim, athletic build. Both Marty and Jimmy, like their father Dick, seemed perennially tanned from being outdoors, and we later learned they liked to camp. Marty's whole demeanor was usually one of annoyance. I used to think that he was just annoyed or irritated with *me,* but now I think he was irritated with the world in general. I have never understood what his problem was, and probably only ever exchanged a few abrupt sentences with him.

Suzie was a tomboy. I always liked Suzie, who never said much but the plain truth, who laughed at times with such freedom, and would have made a great friend to me but was a few years younger and so out of my immediate social circles in school. I recall Suzie with the same sort of puzzled, surprised expression of her mother; blond hair, brown eyes, small, wearing oversized, boyish clothes and baseball caps. She liked animals, and sometimes nursed strays.

One Saturday night not long after we met the Monroes, my parents left my oldest brother Joe and my sister Mary to babysit the rest of us while they went out with Faith and Dick to the Bail Fund Ball held at an old mansion in Cleveland called The Franklin Castle. Father B and a coalition of churches and community groups from the near west side hosted this dance to raise money to help people incarcerated for petty offenses who could not raise bail. Well, it was no secret that the Cleveland Police didn't like Father B and viewed him as a troublemaker. This Bail Fund Ball probably burned their asses. Helping criminals and thieves?

When my parents arrived back home earlier than we'd expected that night, they told us this story. The Cleveland Police raided The Bail Fund Ball. My mother described cops charging into the Franklin Castle in riot gear, swinging billy clubs and using unnecessary force. A black woman hauled off and kicked one of them in the shin. That was it for my parents—they hit the floor running. A bunch of people, Faith and Dick included, got arrested, as did Father B. The reason? He hadn't obtained a liquor license for the event. Now granted, it was the law, but I have no doubts that some of these cops didn't mind cracking heads. It was that era.

That summer after we met the Monroes, my mother announced that we were going camping. Two of my three younger brothers were still toddlers in diapers. This vacation definitely wouldn't be a restful getaway vacation for my parents. I helped my mother put together a tub for dishwashing, plastic utensils, paper plates, a coffee pot, dishcloths, paper towels, and toilet paper. We packed food in coolers with ice, soft drinks, snacks, and stacks of diapers for the baby, real diapers (my mother never used Pampers). My oldest brother Joe helped my dad buy a Coleman stove, lantern, and a used ten man tent, as well as a small, barrel-like cooler that dispensed cold drinks when you pushed a button, quite a novelty. Only a few of the eight of us owned sleeping bags, a popular Christmas gift item at this time, but we took all the sleeping bags we *did* have, plus pillows, blankets, bathing suits, clothes to wear for 2 or 3 days, and fishing poles and tackle. All this, and eight children, were crammed into an orange VW bus with my parents, and off we went for the July 4th, 1974 weekend.

I'm not even sure I knew we were going camping with the Monroes. I just knew we were going somewhere and I had to help my mother prepare. We arrived at the campground on that Friday night after a two hour drive. It was called Catawba, after the kind of grapes that grow in the region, and before that, I think, the Native Americans who lived there. Catawba was located on Lake Erie near Cedar Point and East Harbor in Ohio. Since I'd never been camping before, I didn't realize that Catawba was a rinky-dink little campground as close as possible to civilization as you could get. We could see the main road we'd driven on to get there from our camping site. Anyway, none of us had ever been this close to sleeping in the wilderness, so it was adventure enough.

I had nothing to do with setting up the tent. I ran somewhere to get out of doing any work, and anyway, my older brothers and father liked to do that kind of stuff. I learned later that not only did the Monroes have a tent and all these things we had, they had a sort of day tent made of mesh you could see through. They could go inside and escape the bugs in some shade. They also had two large unwieldy white rectangular coolers made of plastic, like the plastic used to hold gallon jugs of milk, for cold water anytime.

A small stream or inlet from the lake passed by near our campsite. We could easily hop over it, and beyond that on the edge of the campground was a little playground with a swing set and a slide. Not much, but something to do when we weren't swimming or hiking.

We didn't see much of the Monroes that first night at the campground. Either Mr. Monroe and his sons came later after he finished work, or my family must have been overwhelming to them—we were entirely self-sufficient and content to amuse ourselves amongst ourselves and had been for as long as I could remember. Sure, my older sister had begun to go off on her own with older friends and I wasn't always invited, but when we were all together, we had adventures just because there were so many of us. The probability of hijinks and stories to retell later increased exponentially with every child. Perhaps Dickie, Jimmy, Marty and Suzie felt a little shy in our midst—who wouldn't? I remember that first night being with only my family around the campfire, and the fact that I grew hysterical on account of June bugs.

We ate our dinner of hotdogs and hamburgers, and after finding sticks, toasted and feasted on burnt marshmallows. The sun began to set, and my older brothers Joe and John started a campfire, and the rest of us added logs and kindling when the flames dwindled. I was given the assignment, with Mary, to help watch the little ones. I was always nervous about my little brothers and sisters. I think I was more vigilant than my mother about them. I couldn't really help it; I've always had a free-floating anxiety problem. I feared their falling into the campfire, or falling off piers. Anyway, we were all enjoying the darkness and the fire, excited to be sleeping outside in a few hours, happy to be away from home and four walls. This was a new experience for all of us...and it was summer, and it was that time before we noticed ourselves much. It was in being around others, outside of our tribe, when we became self-conscious.

I was sitting in a lawn chair, my arms on the armrests, staring into the fire and the glowing faces of my siblings. Something I couldn't see, something decidedly unhuman, clamped around my right index finger and held on for dear life. I shrieked as if I were being murdered, jumped up, and ran in circles. Mary came to my aid.

"What the matter?"

"There's something on my finger!"

"Well, shake it off."

I tried. "It won't let go!" I screamed some more. My heart raced erratically. In darkness I tried to see. All I could make out was a dark brown shiny thing about the half the size of my finger. The thing moved. Is there anything less human than a beetle? The hard shell, the weird firm underbelly, the clicky little legs, aaaaahhhhh. I felt terror, terror of the alien, the insect, who wears its skeleton on the outside.

"Throw it in the fire!" Mary commanded. I usually, if not always, listened to her. She was older than me and knew more. I tried to shake it into the fire and finally succeeded, but was left shivering, laughing one moment, crying the next. My brothers laughed at me and poked the cremated June bug with a long stick.

Then another June bug landed in my little sister Jennifer's hair. She screamed and shook her head from side to side to get rid of it. I looked up. They were coming from the tall spindly trees around our campsite. That was enough for me. I was going to bed. Still shaking, I unzipped the tent, climbed in, carefully zipped it back up, and climbed into my sleeping bag. Just let those June bugs try to get at me in here. In moments, I was asleep.

That night I am told I dozed restfully through a severe and earsplitting thunderstorm, one that uprooted the stakes of the tent and sent most of my family outside to prevent its blowing away. The rain soaked almost everything so that in the morning we had to take our sleeping bags outside to dry. Soon the sun was strong, the skies clear again, and so a few of the sleeping bags had already dried. My mother told me to roll them up and put them on higher ground near our site until the tent had aired out. I obeyed, and then used them as a sort of couch. I sat down and turned my blue AM transistor radio to a station that was playing top 40 hits. The biggest ones at the time were "Tell Me Something Good" by Rufus and "Band on the Run" by Paul McCartney and the Wings. Chaka Khan sang while I read a book in the late morning heat and waited for the time after lunch when we would all go swimming in the lake.

This was when Jimmy Monroe appeared and plopped down with me on the sleeping bags, with Chaka moaning, "Tell me that you laaheek eeet, yeaaah." I didn't feel self-conscious because I hadn't begun to think much about myself yet. I wish I could go back to those days. The short brown hair my mother had permed against my wishes had begun to turn gold and amber in the summer sun and chlorine from the swimming pool. My skin tanned easily, and was very brown. One thing I particularly loved about myself was the long silky blond hair that grew on my calves. Still, I wasn't sure what to make of Jimmy sitting down with me. I certainly didn't think he was paying me special attention at first. That's how it is when you're young and don't know anything. He wore what we called a muscle shirt back then, which is a sort of sleeveless t-shirt, but more than sleeveless, it has huge openings for the arms. I don't think it telegraphs "white trash" today, but maybe it still does? Well, if Jimmy was some kind of white trash, I would have dared any girl to say she minded. He was from a rougher neighborhood, which I *now* know means he and his friends were more sexually active and experienced at a younger age. But he sat down on the sleeping bags and scooted close to look at my blue transistor radio, casually sneaking an arm around me. I held my breath and didn't move a muscle. If I hadn't been tanned I would have flushed scarlet. I wasn't sure that I liked whatever this was. I needed to breathe so I couldn't continue to hold my breath, but I could hardly summon the courage to speak to him or look him in the eyes! So I stole glimpses of him: long hair falling forward, the profile of his sharp nose, the unreadable blue eyes shaded with black eyelashes looking down at my radio. I tried to figure out what it was that he wanted, and suddenly it dawned on me (mistakenly, I later realized) that it was me! ME he wanted from me! I'm not certain if we spoke. I just stared at my radio in-between glancing at him, and tried unsuccessfully not to giggle.

Is there a better time than to be a girl who isn't aware of her power to attract male attention? Well, those days were over for me after this. What a wonderful thing to be unselfconscious. Jimmy was just a curious boy who didn't own a transistor radio and wanted to see mine. His nature involved exploring and conquering his immediate environment. Curiosity and dominance, that's all it was. But now as then, I have a tendency to romanticize biological motives and drives. Jimmy received the genes necessary to show dominance among other males, and to procreate. Out of the three Monroe boys, he was the only one to have children and continue the Monroe bloodline.

As quickly as he landed there next to me like a June bug, he was gone again.

I wandered away from our campsite, over the creek, to the swings. They had well-worn wooden seats, with smooth grooves that wouldn't leave splinters on your hands, not the bendy plastic kind that wrapped around and squeezed your behind into a U shape and were uncomfortable, confining. But I discovered enormous puddles from last night's storm in the ditches under the swings. I'd need to hop in the seat without stepping in the muddy puddle, and get the swing started without using my feet. I'd have to use my body's weight and my arms to pull and push back and forth with the chains. Occasionally shoving off the ground in the dirt to the sides of the puddles with my feet, rather awkward and hard on the knees. Once I had movement, I could begin to use my legs as long as I wasn't too close to the ground. I liked to swing, though, so I eventually managed to get up pretty high. Then the problem was stopping without raking my sneakers through the rainwater. There were only two swings on this swing set, and an open space where there had been a third, but no more. I'd been swinging for a few minutes when Jimmy reappeared and began to swing next to me.

"I dare you to jump." He quickly managed to swing as high as me.

"You first."

"It's easy. Watch." He swung back, then as he came forward, he let go of the chains and ejected himself with the movement of the swing. He landed a few feet away from the swing set, squatted to regain his balance, and stood up.

"See?"

"Okay." Not wanting to be outdone or called a chicken, I swung back and forth a few times, took a deep breath, and let go. It's the closest I've ever come to flying. My hair rose in the air, I felt weightless, but my legs and feet were sure beneath me, waiting to come back to earth, and I wasn't so heavy that the impact hurt. I landed, fell forward, and stood up, laughing.

"That was fun!"

"Let's do it again."

I wasn't as enthusiastic as Jimmy. I was sure that I would get hurt at some point, but I agreed. We repeated our jumps and after a while I wasn't afraid anymore. At some point Marty came to watch us from nearby, but he didn't speak, just kind of slunk around and scowled. Slowly a few of my brothers and sisters came to watch and take their turns when I'd finally tired of it and Jimmy had stopped to sit under a tree in the shade. I wished he would ask me to sit by him, but he didn't. Dickie strolled up smiling nonsensically, his arms crossed, keeping to himself. Mary took her turn, her long black hair pulled back in a ponytail, a few stray wisps falling out as she landed and claimed one time was enough. She walked back to the campsite where it was almost time for lunch, brushing her dirty hands off on her shorts. Marty claimed he'd jumped off at a higher point than Jimmy, which started an argument between them as to who had jumped higher and farther. I think that was the substance of their entire relationship, in a nutshell. A pissing contest.

We went swimming in the lake that afternoon. John and Joe dug a big hole under two feet of water, which was possible in the lakebed because of the gentle wave action that didn't fill a hole with sand or erode one's handiwork as quickly as ocean waves do. After they dug the hole, they moved away and watched as people, most notably fat women, waded laboriously back towards the shore and stumbled in their invisible ditch. Then they laughed and laughed, squatting down like imps with their faces next to the water.

Jimmy and Marty threw sandy muck from the bottom of the lake at each other. Feeling a need to intentionally guarantee myself Jimmy's continued attention, I joined the battle. Unfortunately, I underestimated my aim and strength. I hit Marty squarely in the face, filling his mouth with ooze from the polluted depths of Lake Erie. Then he started bellowing, and I was afraid his mother would yell at me, but Faith wasn't like that. I just couldn't ever hit it off with Marty no matter how much I wanted to.

On our last night at the campsite, the adults agreed that we would all go out to eat. Now, my father sometimes brought home Arthur Treacher's Fish and Chips, and once I remember going to a Chinese Restaurant called Chung Wah's when an older, engaged cousin came to visit with her fiancé. But other than that my family had little experience with going anywhere more fancy than McDonald's or Dairy Queen, and even then we stayed in the car to eat.

When my father took us to get ice cream, there were so many of us that he simply asked my oldest brother and sister to watch us as he went in. Then he bought chocolate cones for my male siblings and vanilla for the girls; that was how he remembered who got what. I would rather have had chocolate but it never occurred to me to ask.

Well, that whole "eating out" experience proved to be a disastrous disappointment whose consequence may have been Jimmy and Marty Monroe's lasting dislike of my family, and namely, me. I wanted them to like me, but because of our large family, we'd proved to be uncool in their eyes. This shocked me. Didn't they know who we were, who I was? Didn't they know that where we went to school at St. Clement's, we were beloved by all, teachers and students alike?

Dickie and Suzie drove to dinner with us in our van. My mother sat on a crate in the back near us; I sat next to Suzie, who sat next to my sister Mary, who had the window. We'd removed the middle seat from the van so that we could fit more in when we packed. Nobody worried about child safety seats or seat belts, so my little brothers and sisters were crammed in with foodstuffs and assorted necessaries like my mother's Kotex stuffed somewhere in between diapers and toilet paper. How we all managed to fit, in addition to Suzie and Dickie, I have no idea. Now Dickie faced us, sitting on a box by the sliding door. While we sat there waiting for my father and oldest brother Joe to get in the front seats and drive away, Dickie remarked to no one in particular, "I wonder if Mary has had her period yet."

Suzie, though younger than me, seemed to have a much better grasp of reproduction at her nine years than me at eleven. After a moment of shocked silence in which both my mother and my sister Mary's mouths fell open simultaneously, I had taken longer to process what had been said. Yet Suzie gasped, "What? What did you say? Dickie!"

"I wonder if Mary has had her period yet."

"Dickie! God!" Suzie shook her head and started to laugh. Mary closed her mouth and looked bewildered. My mother looked down and frowned, not so much at Dickie but at not knowing how to respond or correct him, and probably also kicking herself for not hiding the Kotex better. I knew Dickie had crossed a boundary, but although I knew a period was blood that only women had, I didn't really understand much else very well. Except, that it was something that even my sister and I didn't talk about unless whispering, and it was always about who had had theirs and who still hadn't. Yes, I figured, it was a pretty personal topic. I looked at Suzie, she looked at me, and we laughed and laughed. Nobody said anything else. Eventually even Mary started laughing because we were facing Dickie, his arms crossed as usual, and it was very uncomfortable not to do something to take the pressure out of the atmosphere of that VW, which was like a big orange balloon about to burst. When we finally stopped laughing, Suzie just shook her head again, and nothing more was said about that subject on our way to dinner.

We pulled up into the gravel parking lot of a long, chrome-trimmed rectangular building. I guess you'd call it a fancy diner, with an attractive sign that glowed a faint pink "Kenny's Restaurant" in the early dusk hours of July. Pleasant and friendly looking enough, it was a seafood restaurant, and nobody in my family had ever been to one. Hungry and excited, we piled out of our van and into the air conditioning while Mr. and Mrs. Monroe, Jimmy and Marty pulled up behind us in their station wagon

The restaurant smelled like French fries. A few couples eating there glanced up at us, and I wasn't sure where to sit as we ventured into the dining room and headed for a row of tables. We'd barely sat down when we realized something was wrong. I'm not sure if my parents didn't come inside with us, or exactly how the message was telegraphed to me, but it turned out we were not staying at Kenny's Restaurant. Those of us who had sat down got back up. We all went back out to the van and got in. A few of us asked questions but I don't recall receiving an answer as to why we weren't staying, and I don't recall where we actually ended up eating. Or if we did even go out somewhere else that night. I just know when I asked Suzie what had happened later, that Jimmy put his finger to his lips and "ssshhhed" her. That's how I figured out that there was something to be ashamed of. My father or mother or both had found the restaurant to be too expensive for ten people, and this was deeply embarrassing. Perhaps hunger sharpened this memory for me, disappointed hunger.

We went on to visit my father's sister and parents in Pennsylvania after the weekend. My father's sister Corinne, who battled epilepsy her whole life, lived with them in Johnsonburg. We loved to visit Nuni, Grandpa, and Aunt Corinne because we always ate well there. Unfortunately, on this visit we all got sick with stomach flu that my mother attributed to either swimming in a polluted lake or camping next to a sewer. But when we returned home, much of the summer still stretched before us.

Each of my brothers and sisters (except our youngest brothers who couldn't yet swim) bought a swimming pass that gave us entrance at two public pools in Lakewood. We sewed the metal pass, a different color every year, onto our bathing suits. Then wrapped them in a towel, carried the rolled up towel under our arms, and walked the ten blocks to change into our suits at Madison, the pool closest to our house. My older brothers Joe and John, who made money from paper routes, bought their own bikes, and could secure them with locks at the pool. Most families owned only one car, and my father drove ours the thirty miles to his job and back on the east side of Cleveland. So if we wanted to go somewhere, we walked, rode a bike, or took a bus.

Madison Pool was a little smaller than the one at Lakewood Park, but it had a separate diving area, ten feet deep with two lower diving boards on each side of a high board. There were times, jumping off that high board, that I seriously wondered if I was going to die. Once I watched Marty Monroe do a sailor's dive off the high board. Standing precariously at the very edge of the board, he bent over, grabbed his ankles, and sort of fell off the board head first. He was so brave! The larger swimming area went from three to six feet and back down to three feet again. This larger pool featured a slide area separated by floating, white plastic bubbles on ropes. Bubble ropes also separated the deeper six foot area from the two three-four foot areas. One could dive in the six feet but only jump in the three.

The pool was a daily part of our summer routine as long as the weather was good and even sometimes when it wasn't. We didn't need much but the sight of a curly white slide suspended over teal-colored water to become excited. It looked as happy as candy. Brightly colored bathing suits, white bubbles bobbing on the surface, the smell of chlorine, tanning oil and popcorn. Forty-five minutes of exhaustive running and jump-ing and diving and splashing and playing and doing tricks in the sunshine, and then the whistle stopped us for a break. Then drying off a bit, and getting hot again, and waiting in the growing heat for the whistle to sound. So, oh sweet release, we could jump into the cooling water, and the noise and splashing continued. For hours. Until it was almost dinner time. There was no snack bar at the pool, so after getting dressed again and walking home with ears slightly off due to water, our stomachs felt like aching empty caverns and we were starving to eat. Food always tasted so good after all that exercise. Sometimes we went back to the pool again after dinner. Then the sun had lost its power, and the tired air was almost a hazy orange in the dusk. The pool still offered relief, though the water was warm from a day in the sun and a little cloudy from tanning oil.

I soon found out that summer that the Monroes went swimming at Madison Pool. I discovered too, that I was beneath their attention, beneath speaking to at the pool or anywhere else. What *they* didn't know was that *I* knew their every move when they were at the pool even as I pretended not to.

Jimmy wore a red bathing suit. Marty wore brown. They didn't often appear together, if ever. Mostly Marty showed up without Jimmy. If I was interested in Marty, I had competition, at least in my own mind. Somehow, I knew I wasn't even in the running, but I could dream.

From my observations I learned that when a girl named Robin was at the pool, boys like Marty swarmed around and flirted with her by threatening to push her in the water. Robin had the body I coveted: long slim legs, small ass, large breasts, (in sixth grade) a cute, angular face that later photographed well in our high school yearbook, and curly brown hair. She wore a simple, blue, one-piece bathing suit, so I couldn't character-assassinate her for being a show-off or provocative. On the surface, Robin seemed to have it all going on. I was slightly overweight and wore hand me downs, although I had bought a cool red tank, the kind real Olympic swimmers wore, from the sporting goods store that year, and I had a nice tan, and a brand new red, white and blue striped beach towel Joe had given me for my birthday. Madison stopped requiring bathing caps, so I ditched mine.

Seeing Marty or Jimmy at the pool always provided a bright spot in my day, something to look forward to. Jimmy probably had bigger fish to fry elsewhere most of the time. But the following anecdote sums up my non-relationship, my non-even-friendship with Marty Monroe, despite the fact that he definitely knew who I was, and had spent a weekend camping with me.

One day I went to the pool as usual with my friends. I knew from my Marty radar that he was across the pool from me at one point as I stood waiting for some-one to move so I could dive into the six feet. I watched surreptitiously as he ran from the fence bordering the concrete deck that surrounded the pool, a distance of some ten feet, leapt into the air three-four feet away from the side of the pool; hit the water about three-four feet off the side (not waiting, as I did, for an open space because he could somehow change directions in mid-flight); swam underwater like a seal for the approximately 50 yards across the pool; and surfaced directly at my feet where I stood at the edge. I smiled down at him with goofy admiration, but he just threw his head back, shaking the hair out of his eyes so that it lay plastered to his forehead like a piece of seaweed.

He squinted up into the direct sunlight at me standing there, in his way, and made both a face and a sound of disgust as he pulled himself out of the water to my side, water streaming behind him.

What did it mean? Those rejections, though hard to stomach, taught me to act like I didn't care. I learned to remain deep inside of myself where few could ever reach me. Marty Monroe didn't teach me that. He was one of many who taught me that in adolescence. If you might hurt me, then I wouldn't ever really let you know who I was. Problem was, I didn't know either. But how else could one survive?

Flash forward to 1979. I was in high school and miserable. I wasn't one of those people for whom high school marked the climax of their existence. I went with a girlfriend to the gym to watch a basketball game, the strategy of which made a lot more sense to me than football. I experienced walking past the hundreds of other students in the gym bleachers as painful. I was afraid. I was cautious. I'd seen how people could be mean, and people had been mean to me, mostly other girls, even when I tried to be friendly. I'll never forget Eileen Collins rolling her eyes and popping a bubble, insinuating that I was gay when I gave her and a few other girls in my freshman civics class a cheap super-market Valentine, the kind that come 30 to a box. I never did *that* again. I went to parochial schools for eight years, up through junior high, but wanted to go to a public high school and didn't realize that it might be difficult to make the transition from private to public school where most of the other students already knew at least a few people. My class of 1981 alone had nearly 900 students. Add to that, I was pretty much a dork, and oversensitive. I attended the "smart" classes, and I liked theater, the main reason I chose this school. But the theater group was probably the only one that took anyone who wanted to join, and was thus filled with misfits and dorks like myself. I didn't care. I had a serious dream. My career path, the way I saw it, depended on my doing as much theater as possible at this school to hone my skills before either attending a theater school or joining a repertory theater. I would do anything to show my dedication, including building sets for *Arsenic and Old Lace* my freshman year. Never mind that a teenage boy made up to look like an old man wasn't convincing to anyone in the audience. I was serious, I meant business, I was going places, and I told myself that this time in high school represented a mere step-ping stone. It didn't really matter to me, for I had a direction and plan to move far away from this place, from these barbarians and Philistines, and become successful. I'm not sure what exactly happened to this person that I was back then, but that's another story.

This night presented a different sort of theater. I sat on a hard wooden bench in a gym that smelled like sweat a hundred years old. Outside it was winter. We'd walked, my friend and I, through ice and snow to get there. None of us could drive yet, and who had a car anyway? We kept our coats on. We wore jeans or corduroy Levis, which we bought ourselves with money we earned babysitting because we weren't yet sixteen.

The teams ran out and jumped for the ball. That's when I noticed Jimmy. I had no idea he made the varsity basketball team because I wasn't what you'd call "in the loop" socially. But, someone who looked like Jimmy Monroe appeared on the court in our gold and purple Lakewood High School Rangers uniform, old-style, back when the shorts were still short. Only Jimmy managed to dignify this costume. Not a spare ounce of fat on his long body. Like so many young athletes, he looked divine, angelic, God-like. I wasn't drooling over him as I watched. I felt in awe of him. His smooth flesh glowed with the circulation of oxygen-rich blood. Jimmy with the dirty mustache on his lip, the long, swinging brown hair, stalked the ball and navigated the court with catlike stealth. Well. There he was again, Big Man On Campus. And to think that he once wooed me on a rolled up sleeping bag.

I graduated from high school and went to college far away, married, and had children. In the course of many trips home to see my parents, I heard the following stories about the Monroes.

Dickie joined the military, the navy. One day he came over with Faith and Dick to visit my parents.

When my father said, "Hello, Dickie," he said, "I'd prefer to be called Richard."

My father answered, "O.K., Dickie."

Jimmy either married or didn't marry, but nevertheless fathered a child with one of the women he ran with in high school. I think they most often lived with Faith and Dick on their frequent moves around the country. I heard at various times that they lived in Utah, then the Chesapeake Bay area of Maryland, then back in Ohio. At some point, the mother of Jimmy's daughter left, taking the baby and starting a custody battle. At another time, Jimmy stole the baby back. The Monroes continued to move around like nomads.

Were they avoiding the law or something? We had no idea; in any case, we had no evidence. But I listened to my mother's stories. Marty was a car salesman. Suzie had become a paramedic.

Then Dickie died of some kind of heart failure way before his time while visiting Faith and Dick. He'd gone out to sit on the end of their pier on Chesapeake Bay and suffered an attack without any warning. When they found him, he wasn't breathing.

Now Dick and Faith were living back in Cleveland with Jimmy and the little girl. Faith had been diagnosed with ovarian cancer. She was doing okay, though. She was in the hospital. Then she was back home. She painted watercolors, mostly flowers, and when my mother asked her for one, Faith gave her a painting of some purple irises. I kept a framed picture of the two of them from this time, Faith in the foreground, looking surprised that someone was taking her picture. My mother stood behind her, eyes magnified behind bifocals, looking hesitant. They looked like two little girls caught in the act of stealing candy.

Next I heard that Faith was very ill and had to go into the hospital again. My mother wasn't sure she would be coming home this time. She visited her, and called on Jimmy and Dick with meals, offering help and support, but Jimmy was always very protective of Faith and rejected my mother's offers. I had a theory about this.

After our camping trip so many years before, there'd been an incident, a conflict between Jimmy and my mother. When we traveled on to our grand-parents in Pennsylvania after the three-day July 4th weekend, the Monroes drove back to Lakewood. We returned home later the following weekend, and my mother went over to the Monroes' house to bring them some beach towels that had been left in our car. Faith and Dick weren't home, so she left the towels with Jimmy, who had answered the door. As she was leaving, Jimmy asked her if we had one of their two water coolers; they were large and unwieldy, opaque, white rectangular containers two feet deep and about 3 feet long, with red spigots. It seemed one of their coolers was missing, and the Monroes thought, or at least Jimmy thought, we, namely my mother, had taken it. Not only would my mother never have stolen anything from any-one, the cooler was large. She, all of us, certainly would have noticed if we had mistakenly taken it. In addition to which, the cooler would definitely not have fit in our VW with eight children, two adults, all our clothing, towels, sleeping bags, tent, stove, lantern, etc. My mother said as much to Jimmy.

"You must have taken it," Jimmy insisted.

"But Jimmy, I don't *have* it," my mother answered, hurt at his insinuation.

She came home, troubled, and told me what had passed between them. I didn't think much of it at the time except that I vaguely felt it was another strike against us along with the restaurant incident. Also, I wasn't sure if my mother didn't deserve some punishment even if she wasn't guilty, because: 1. we famously didn't get along; 2. she had force-permed my hair, and 3. she had eight children and thus was either banned from or couldn't afford to go out to seafood restaurants. I was a pre-teen, a daughter, and highly critical of her at that time and for many years after.

Faith died. I lived far away from home then, but I did send her husband Dick a card. My parents went to the funeral and to Dick and Faith's house for a gathering afterwards. That my mother loved Faith, I have no doubt. But there was Jimmy, a roadblock to acknowledging any feeling of intimacy or friendship between them. He wouldn't let my mother get close to him, to comfort him. Now that I think of it, the poor boy was probably so possessive of Faith, and so devastated that he could think only in terms of what he had lost: the most important woman in his life. In the same way, I suppose, my mother lost her favorite friend, and it only occurred to me much later how that must have felt, and how little real sympathy I gave to her when it happened.

Seven or eight years passed where I heard little about the Monroes. Then one day toward the end of October three years ago, my mother called to tell me some terrible news. Apparently Dick and Jimmy had gone on a trip to the Caribbean, and had been found dead, drowned. I imagined they'd chartered a boat and planned to do some deep sea fishing together, perhaps some snorkeling and scuba diving. Their bodies washed ashore on a beach in Costa Rica. There was trouble notifying next of kin and getting the bodies shipped back to the States. I don't know how Suzie or Marty heard the awful news. Did they have to go down to Central America to identify them? From what I heard from my brother John, who went to the funerals, neither Marty nor Suzie knew many details. Did one of them get into trouble in the water, and the other, making the biggest mistake in lifeguard water safety rules, jump in to save him, and also drown? Did Dick have a heart attack in the water, and Jimmy tried to retrieve his body? Did their boat get swamped with waves during a storm out at sea? Were they washed or thrown overboard? It would be unlikely that they were involved in some kind of illegal activity like drug running, or had seen something they weren't supposed to see, and became victims of homicide. It was telling to me, though, that Marty wasn't with his father and brother. All families have their strange dynamics, and I guessed that Marty learned to stay out of the middle of Faith and Jimmy as soon as he could. Maybe the mother of Jimmy's little girl had done the same.

I was left with an image in my mind of crests of white foam surging on tongues of teal-colored water to the bleached sand of a tropical beach. But for the constant blast of wind and water and seagulls crying, there was otherwise only silence. Father and son came to rest in separate places on the shore of paradise, nudged by waves, entangled in seaweed. It was so hot, the sun an unforgiving eye in the heavens. A boat anchored somewhere offshore, awaiting their return, rocked and creaked with the motion of the sea.

I went back home to Lakewood last weekend to celebrate Father's Day with my family. What I learned in asking my parents questions about the Monroes and what happened years ago is a testament to the creativity of my memory. I'm left wondering about the reliability of my recollections.

My mother met Faith at a meeting in Lakewood, not down at Father B's community on the near west side of Cleveland, although they eventually did volunteer work together there. Faith invited my parents to her house, and for a long time, Dick used to sit in a corner and not say anything.

My mother didn't recall Father B having long hair. The church where Father B said Mass was St. Coleman's, not St. Malachi's. St. Coleman's was where Suzie and Marty said goodbye to Faith, Dick and Jimmy.

The reason we had to leave the restaurant on our camping trip with the Monroes was because it was an adult lounge and they didn't want to wait on twelve children. This was my mother's story, but I questioned why Jimmy would blame my family and not his, as if the waitress would wait on the four Monroe children and not us. Because he was being a jerk?

And finally, although there were no witnesses, a rip tide most likely drowned Jimmy and Dick. They weren't on a boat but staying at a place on the beach down in Costa Rica where Dick wanted to retire. I don't know where I came up with scuba diving, deep sea fishing, snorkeling, or storms, etc. Wait. Yes I do. That's the kind of outdoorsmen they were.

But I'm ambivalent. Is it really just an indication of my brain's need to create reasonable stories without enough information, or do I remember correctly? Was it my mother who rewrote the story? I'll never know.

BONANZA

The skin of the sunken chest under Aunt Mary's pink nightgown was brown and speckled, like an egg. To be honest, it made me think of the pictures of mummies I'd seen, dried out and ancient. On Sundays I sat with the bedridden old woman while her niece Lucille attended 11 o'clock Mass. I gave Aunt Mary coffee, or a soft-boiled egg, and struck matches to light her cigarettes.

Lucille said it was her last pleasure.

Lucille kept her aunt's long white hair pulled up and back into a messy bun that she sometimes roughly brushed in haste, if a priest or a layperson came to give Aunt Mary Holy Communion. Then Aunt Mary's face showed the squashed, irritated expression of a cat suffering unwanted petting. A few times when Lucille fixed it, I saw Aunt Mary's hair down. First I thought: ghost. On further reflection, stealing glimpses of her, she looked like a pretty little girl. Once when Lucille asked me to come so she could get groceries, and had lumbered down the steep second floor duplex stairs, the hem of her skirt partly undone, to the cab waiting in the street, Aunt Mary said, "Oh baby. I thought

she'd never leave." She spoke haltingly, having suffered a few strokes. Surprised, I laughed. The mummy
had a personality and a sense of humor.

The first few times I sat with Aunt Mary, I had to
lift her to a portable potty kept right next to her high
hospital bed. Both bed and potty sat smack in the center of the living room. Aunt Mary encircled my neck
and held on with her long arms, which though frail,
seemed graceful, and I'd put my hands under her armpits and lift her, maneuvering her from where she sat at
the side of the bed to the potty. Then she managed to sit
her 90 pounds down, and I would leave the room for a
while to give her privacy. A few minutes later I'd check
back on her, and when she said, "I'm ready," I helped
her back into bed again. Positioning a frail, ninety-
pound woman on her pillows so that she retained a
certain dignity in her posture amongst the bedclothes
presented no simple feat for a young woman of fifteen, only about 100 pounds herself. Arranging her
left me feeling guilty, as if I were merely displaying
the limbs of a lifeless doll without regard to how the
doll felt about having her body manipulated. She was
nearly powerless to do anything about it.

Later, when Aunt Mary no longer got up out
of bed to use the portable toilet but took a bedpan,

I had to help her hoist her thighs and behind, and once I accidentally glimpsed grey hair between her legs. It wasn't so repulsive, but I recall her sideways glance at me, to read my reaction. Once she took my hands in hers until I looked at her—the light in her glittering black eyes implored me to see her, so she could smile and say, "Aren't you lovely." Startled by her lucidity—we rarely talked—and by a fleeting sense that we were looking at our own reflections, I returned her gaze, reluctantly at first. I didn't respond well to praise, and had no idea how lovely I was, nor that I might ever resemble Aunt Mary. Impossible. The room smelled of Desitin and talcum powder to prevent bedsores, and the smoke from her cigarettes. On winter days when Lucille blasted the heat, the atmosphere in the room grew oppressive to me, and hours after I'd left I could still smell those things.

Once when I removed the bedpan from under Aunt Mary, I discovered it was full of at least three pounds of tarry stool that smelled worse than anything I had ever smelt. I tried to keep my eyes from widening in shock and horror as I bore the bedpan over my head and away into the bathroom where, gagging, I spent fifteen minutes rinsing out contents that had taken weeks to flush from her bowels. I almost threw up.

Aunt Mary liked to watch Bonanza reruns. Back then the actor who played Hoss was already dead, and Michael Landon, who played Little Joe, soon would be. I began to sneak cigarettes when Aunt Mary fell asleep during the show, and smoked them in the kitchen, where I sat at a small table covered with newspapers and crumbs.

Lucille brought me a few dollars and some treats from her grocery trips: bear claws and cheesecake, bags of expensive jellied candy. Sometimes she gave me a piece of gaudy jewelry I never wore.

"She's going to be a nurse, Aunt Mary," Lucille shouted in her ear when I said goodbye.

"What's that?"

"Are you going to be a nurse?" Lucille asked, turning to me.

"No. I want to be an actress."

"Oh. Lovely." Aunt Mary raised a shaky hand. "See how...steady? Can I have a...a cigarette?" She pronounced it "see-gah-ray-ette."

One day when Lucille had left for church wearing a fur coat that grew shabbier each year, Aunt Mary called out to me and I went to her side. She grabbed my wrist, pulled me close.

"I know you take the cigarettes," she said. "I've seen you."

I froze where I stood bent over her.

"Go ahead! I'm not going to tell Lucille."

I didn't know what to do. She'd caught me in the act of stealing from her. I looked at the ground, refused to meet her eyes. "I'm sorry," I said.

I took a job selling doughnuts at a bakery on weekend mornings and never went back.

A few years later I heard Aunt Mary had died. My mother began to invite Lucille to Sunday dinner. My father drove her to church and back on snowy days and helped her up and down our steps. Lucille wore a blue knit hat that was the cornflower color of her eyes, which had grown cloudier. Once when I told her how beautiful they were, she smiled and spoke in a singsong way.

"I had my chance once with a young fellow, a soldier, but I pulled a boner." She shrugged, the corners of her mouth turned down, and her voice rose to a cry. "He asked me to marry him and I said I wasn't ready." She shrugged again, stuck out her drooping lower lip and looked away.

What did I care about anybody? I was applying to college, trying to get as far away from my parents, my hometown, and everyone who knew me, so I could become something or someone without hindrance.

That Sunday night I went to the library with a boy from my English class to work on our college entrance essays. I was applying to a prestigious theater school and wrote about my recent performance in *The Diary of Anne Frank*. I wanted to act, I wrote, in order to convey joy, suffering, to make people laugh. My friend Chuck's goals were similarly lofty. He wanted to become a doctor.

"The reason I want to save lives," Chuck read, "is because of an experience I had one night as a hospital orderly. I was walking down a hall when I saw an old woman on a stretcher. She was gasping for air. No one else was around, so I yelled for help and tried to give her mouth to mouth. The nurses came and took her away, and I later learned she'd died that night. I found out her name was Mary Newman. I'll never forget the feeling of wanting to help another human being in that moment, and I'd like to dedicate my life to the care of others."

"You won't believe this," I said. "I used to take care of her when her niece went to church. Aunt Mary."

I didn't see Chuck again until I came home for a high school reunion. He wasn't a doctor. I wasn't an actress. I wasn't even a nurse.

My mother continued to have Lucille over for Sunday dinners and holidays while I was away at school and afterwards. Each year Lucille grew more blind and hard of hearing but she still sat, happy to be among friends, to be served coffee and dessert. These must have been the only times anyone cared for or fussed over her. I remember her last holding a mug of coffee as if it were china, smiling faintly, a guest at a fine hotel instead of sitting in one of our little dining room chairs with worn upholstery.

I learned later that Lucille's remaining relatives finally took control of her living situation, distancing themselves from my concerned parents. In the end, her caretakers neglected her and she died alone.

I have a recurring dream. I'm looking up at Aunt Mary and Lucille's apartment window from the sidewalk below. The light from a television flickers inside and I can hear the theme song from Bonanza over a fan blowing to cool the rooms on sweltering August Sunday mornings.

In the dream I know they are gone. Someone else lives there.

BEING POLISH

I found many things about being Polish that seemed stupid and shameful besides my mother's maiden name "Yopek." My mother's brother, my uncle Stanley, was a professional musician who played the accordion in various bands. But...an accordion? I was all about the Beatles. I hadn't started kindergarten yet when my brother's friends, carrying rakes and brooms for makeshift guitars and microphones, made us chase them as they ran away, singing, "She Loves You, Yah Yah Yah!"

The Polish people's dance? The polka. The polka! Polka sounded almost as bad as Yopek! And guess whose mother was crowned Polka Queen when she'd just finished high school? Sophie Yopek, my mom, that's who. She showed me a faded newspaper clipping from her cedar chest.

But I didn't feel this aversion to my Polish-ness immediately. My self-loathing began when I heard John Macbane tell a Polish joke, in first grade, mind you. He told it over and over.

"How many Polish people does it take to screw in a light bulb?" he asked.

"Five. One to hold the light bulb and the other four to turn him around and around." Of course sometimes someone in the class already knew the joke and blurted out the punchline before John, which for me begged the question: were Polack jokes universally known?

Now John probably heard that joke from his parents. Where I lived, a large portion of the population was Irish. This could be proven by the number of bars with neon shamrock signs or names like Tam O'Shanter or Blarney Stone that dotted Madison and Detroit Avenues in Lakewood. Also, most of my classmates had these names: Murray, Masterson, McNamara, Murphy, Sullivan, Daugherty, Dugan, Gallagher, Flanagan, O'Malley, and Hannah. When I was in first grade, the Gallagher and Dugan sisters came in and did Irish jigs in front of my class on St. Patrick's Day. There were no Yopeks. Multiple families, however distantly related, shared these Irish names. My first boyfriend in seventh grade was Mike Masterson: Irish. In eighth grade, Kevin Hyland gave me a mood ring—he even had an older brother named the exotically Gaelic *Seamus*.

Fate provided me with one great consolation: no one need ever know about my mother's maiden name. My father's, and her married name, was Bianco; thus our neighbors the Giamattis and later anyone Italian—they were *paesan* in my book. If I'd grown up in New Jersey or California, I would have discovered myself to be among a dozen kids with the same common name. "Bianco" sounded much better than Yopek and helped me stand out in a cool way even before the release of "The Godfather." I could thank my Dad that I didn't have to go through life with Yopek hanging around my neck like a lead kielbasa. Although some kids would probably have said, "Yo, Peck!" Instead, schoolmates called me "Bianco," and I was down with that.

Was my shame innate or learned? Were the Polish somehow genetically abject, given the many traumas to the borders and national identity of Poland? I theorized that my shame originated with my mother's own shame issues, which I believe to have been traumatic. Her parents, both Polish peasant immigrants, came to the U.S and passed through Ellis Island in the 1920's. Long before my mother was born, my grandfather, a musician by trade, first worked slaughtering animals by banging their heads with a sledgehammer, and later as a tanner in the meatpacking industry in Chicago. When he married my grandmother, he bought a farm near Ridgeway, Pennsylvania. There my mother was born and lived for 12 years with her three siblings, farming, milking cows, growing their own food and slaughtering their own chickens and livestock. My mother lived most of her childhood without indoor plumbing before moving into town. They were never hungry, but more difficult than their poverty was the language barrier they experienced. At home they spoke Polish. Back then there were no ESL teachers at public schools; on top of that, they lived in the country, isolated from the support of ethnic communities that formed in major cities like New York or Chicago.

In 4th grade I went on a trip with my mother, along with my little brothers and sister Sophie, to Erie where my grandparents lived at the time, to help my mother clean my grandmother's kitchen. We called my Polish grandmother "Muma," which was pronounced exactly as it looks. Muma was born on a farm near Krakow and remembered German soldiers coming to take her family's food during the First World War. When she was eight years old, Muma's mother died of stomach cancer. Her father put her and her brother in an orphanage and went to make his fortune in the United States—with the intention of sending for them later. Mom claimed the reason for Muma's slovenliness was because she never learned anything from the nuns in the orphanage but embroidery, hardly a life skill. (I never thought to ask, "If Muma never learned to clean, how did *you* learn to clean so well?") As we scrubbed away the grime, (jelly hardened on refrigerator surfaces, honey spilled in the pantry, gluing cardboard cartons and ants to the wood shelves), I felt sorry for my grandfather. He sat unresponsive and expressionless in his armchair; a five o'clock shadow smeared across his jowls like axle grease, in a room where, in order to preserve them, Muma covered all the upholstery and part of the carpet with odd smelling sheets of plastic. The whole apartment smelled of mothballs. They lived in a rundown section of Erie, what we called "the slums," close to the downtown area, wherever that was. Muma was a landlord—they owned the place and she rented out the upstairs apartment.

I didn't ask why Tutuh sat there all day in his green armchair covered by a blanket —I just assumed that's what old people did. But he shaved while sitting there, using the Norelco electric razor Mom brought as a present from Dad. I never suspected he was heavily medicated. Once I thought he looked so sad that I gave him a kiss. In response, he said something like

"Otchie" to my grandmother, which is the Polish nickname for his youngest daughter, my aunt Jane. Maybe I reminded him of her. Although I'm not sure how. My aunt Jane was thin and fair, with blond hair, and high, photogenic, Slavic cheekbones. I looked the opposite in every way, which isn't to say I was short, swarthy and fat-faced. I was a brunette, olive-skinned, had a round face with no cheekbones, and was terribly unphotogenic, typically appearing seizure-stricken, eyes fluttering half open, when photographed.

Tutuh eventually went to a state hospital and I never saw him again. When we visited him at the hospital on a few occasions, I wasn't allowed on his floor because I was too young. One day I came home from school to find my mother at the kitchen stove cutting up onions and tossing them into a frying pan with a sizzling slab of meat. Immediately I wondered what I had done wrong, because she remained silent and sullen, keeping her back to me. These were my cues that she was angry, but her anger confused me. I hadn't always done something wrong to cause it—I'd been gone all day! Then she said, "My father died."

"Oh." I felt relieved that she wasn't mad at me, and because this might mean a break from school for a few days. Only then did I think of how she must feel. I tried to read her, but I couldn't tell—did her sadness look like anger?

"I'm so sorry, Mom." I thought the normal behavior in response to this news was for us to hug and comfort each other. But she indicated with stiff, remote body language and by continuing to work at putting dinner on the table that she didn't wish to interact, let alone be touched, and in this manner signaled all of us to stay away from her.

Tutuh's funeral was a grim, lonely affair in a cavernous church on a rainy day in Erie. My impression of Erie was even bleaker than my impression of Cleveland. Dreary. Dreary Erie. Although a smattering of neighbors brought questionable-looking stuffed cabbages and other potluck fair for us to eat afterwards, the few mourners recalled no fond memories of my Polish grandfather. No one told stories of his life or explained anything about Tutuh to me. We were never close, so I knew very little about him and assumed that's just how it went with old people.

From the way we were raised, I assumed Mom was brought up strictly Catholic by her parents, but perhaps that wasn't the case. I think she received her zealous training in Catholicism at St. Leo's High School in Ridgeway, where she was promoted and loved by a few well educated nuns who knew intelligence and potential when they saw it. She had a quick mind, was observant to a fault, and possessed rigorous standards for herself and for her performance in all areas. Perhaps she felt she owed it to the nuns' care and love, to their raising her out of semi-ignorance, to bring up her own children to be the best Catholics she could. For her, this required indoctrinating us in Catholicism with the hopes that we might someday be canonized, because that was the standard in our house. It was not an American Catholicism that I experienced in childhood and adolescence, but a Roman Catholicism of the Inquisition delivered by a woman who was raised in part by an abusive father with mental illness.

Did my mother adhere so fervently to the Catholic faith because she thought that might save her, and us, from the sense that something wasn't quite right in her family? Save us from that "dis-ease?" I sensed that she didn't like spending much time at her house when she was a girl, and instead liked to visit a big family on the next farm, the McDonalds, who taught her how to make fudge and otherwise have fun. Mom must have equated happiness and "normality" with a large family, and dreamt of someday having a big happy family of her own. She eventually got her wish because, for better or worse, there were eight of us.

When he came to the U.S., Tutuh went from being a popular, carefree musician in Poland to employment in menial, mind-numbing, hazardous jobs, eventually a wife and family to support, and hard work on his farm. Mom theorized that Tutuh may have thought Muma's father had money—it was her father he first met in the States and who told him about his daughter Jenny back in Poland. Whether his beliefs about her wealth were delusional, or whether Muma's father led him on to believe there was an Old World "dowry" of sorts, I don't know, but after they were married, when Tutuh found out Muma was penniless, he appeared to behave as if he felt tricked. He didn't need that or any excuse for his tendency to manic depressive paranoia to play an insidious part in his blame of her for all that was wrong in his life. He worked a regular job and continued to play frequent gigs on the side, eventually enlisting his talented son Stan to join him in these musical ventures. But he abused my grandmother, both physically and verbally, something I guessed long before my mother told me, because when Mom raged at me with her "mask" of anger and disgust, I thought I was actually seeing Tutuh reflected in her face.

Mom rarely discussed her hospitalization in Pittsburgh at age six, for a serious illness. Pittsburgh was two hours from her home. Tutuh took her to the hospital and then left her alone there for six weeks. No one explained anything to her; no one visited or called. I'm sure the experience of abandonment was traumatic for my mother, but she claimed she didn't know any better.

A child thinks, "Doesn't everybody go through this?" We either act out, or accept our situations, and tuck any trauma into a corner of the mind to be dealt with much later, if ever. How did she know if Tutuh was coming back to get her? She says she didn't. When she told me about this experience, I began to perceive the roots of her strength, her stubbornness, her ability to survive heartbreak in her lifetime, the mental and physical endurance bordering on mania for some kind of control over her Polish borders, her environment. Because, if my mother was anything, she was a control freak, yet there were methods to her "madness." But how was I supposed to know these things when I was a mere girl?

She told me, "Once you realize you're alone, then you're okay." When I got older I recalled her confiding this to me and thought, "Ah, so she was really an *existentialist* but she didn't know it!"

Mom had a bad temper, and I'm her daughter in this and many other traits I point out in her, but who wouldn't lose their temper with eight children in a tiny house with little help and money? When angry or stressed, a daily if not hourly occurrence, she raged and swore. She called me (and as far as I knew, no one else in my family) *swinia*, the Polish word for "pig," which made sense, because from the moment I emerged from the womb, it was apparent to all those around me that I couldn't get enough of everything good. The situation was exacerbated by heavy competition for a limited amount of resources. Sometimes, if I'd been bad, or if she thought I'd been bad, she called me a bitch, like she was spitting. She said these things at times when she felt pushed beyond the human limits of patience, fatigue, and endurance. But I didn't know that.

One night my sister Grace and I were talking and giggling upstairs in bed with our dolls under the covers, when we should have been asleep. We heard Mom's approach too late—she swooped into our room and hit me on the back with one of her loafers. It made a loud slapping noise even though I was wearing pajamas, and did the trick of silencing both of us. Later, standing on the toilet, craning my neck around to view my back in the bathroom medicine cabinet mirror,

I clearly saw the red imprint of Mom's shoe on my flesh. The physical pain didn't hurt me as much as the fact that Grace escaped Mom's wrath for some reason. I didn't let my sister hear me cry, but I wondered... if she realized Mom hit me and not her, wouldn't she step up and defend me or protest this unfairness? We were both talking when we should have been asleep, after all. But everyone knew I caused trouble, and so the assumption was that I was the instigator.

This was behavior my mother witnessed in her own home, probably by Tutuh. I don't consider it child abuse in the serious sense of the term, even if there were times I wondered if she didn't prefer me dead. She saw her behavior, her rages, as discipline, and must have known I was strong enough to "absorb" such discipline, whereas most of my siblings might have crumbled; at least, that's what I told myself for a long time. I often caused trouble for her when I didn't mean to, and sometimes I appeared to do things to provoke her intentionally. Of course there were many times I did act deliberately, talking back or further provoking her by arguing a point of fairness. Yes, I had a mouth on me. But in some of those instances, I really believed she might listen to reason when I protested.

One might get a sense of how Mom appeared to others outside of our family, like Felicia and Franny, when they came over to my house to play for the first time and solemnly addressed her as "Sir." My mother was a force to be dealt with, who inspired fear and respect, and it's a point of pride with me that I survived childhood, even if at a price.

The parents of friends who lived in my neighborhood had well-paying occupations like truck driver, secretary, welder, printer, and butcher. Many women were stay at home moms who later worked when their kids were in school all day. My father was atypical in that, with mom's help and support, he completed a Bachelor's degree in business, something about which my mother was exceptionally proud. The only accomplishment of which she may have been prouder would be to have graduated from college herself. (She wanted to go, but Tutuh wouldn't help her, so she worked instead.) There was some unspoken expectation, either from my parents, or just between us siblings, that we would attend college. These aspirations weren't universally shared by my elementary and junior high school, or even high school friends, nor were they expected of them. Our neighbors were mostly educated through high school, working class, good people who helped you at the drop of a hat, racist, yes, although fairly harmless. In the absence of experience or education, they harbored certain assumptions, call them prejudices, about people of other cultures that they didn't live near or understand, but in general they wouldn't have hurt anyone out of spite. They certainly "looked down on others" like the rest of us. My family was really no different except that we didn't use the "n" word in our home, as if that proved we weren't racist, or were less racist, but some of those who lived around us did freely. Or they said "colored."

Our neighbors also told Polack jokes. Sometimes these jokes were slyly directed at my family, maybe as payback for what could have been considered "our pretensions." Was it going too far to guess that the neighbors thought we Biancos held ourselves a little more proudly than the rest, because we excelled academically, assumed college was our birthright, and didn't use the "n" word? Maybe some of the neighbor mothers felt Mom was a little too proud of my father, as if his education made him better than their husbands, who used their hands to make a living. Or they may have been jealous of the academic success of her children, especially Joe, while theirs were at best mediocre and at worst serious behavior problems.

Our next door neighbors on each side were German. To our left, Virginia Dehaney, a widow, and her mother, Alice Weber. The Wisewursts lived on the other side of us; and across the street, the Wilhelms and Deutsch's. We were surrounded by the enemy. When the subjects of Germany and Hitler came up in conversation one day when I was twelve and reading *The Diary of Anne Frank* for the first time, a visiting Mrs. Dehaney told me she owned a copy of *Mein Kampf*. I asked Mom if I could read Hitler's book. Mrs. Dehaney looked at my mother, who shook her head, no. But Mrs. Dehaney owned a copy of *Mein Kampf*. That seemed to be almost a Nazi endorsement.

On the other side of us lived the Wisewursts, Inga and Rob and their two children. Inga was overweight and had a loud and prominent northern Ohio nasal accent one heard when she called her children home. They were the kind of people who yelled, "Stay off our grass!" about their postage stamp-sized lawn, but Rob bought every imaginable piece of equipment to refine this turf.

But Muma had taught my mother that the Germans took Poland away from the Poles, took food from the mouths of children on her own farm. Mom grew up in the country long before the practice of any political correctness, where immigrants were often targets for mockery. Now, in Lakewood, she lived sandwiched between two sets of more culturally assimilated German Americans, and across the street from two others. She justifiably felt a little paranoid, surrounded as she was by the old enemy. Sometimes these groups got together and drank on their front porches; talk turned to jokes, and what better than Polack jokes?

One summer evening after dinner, Mom was shaking rugs out against our front porch banister. I couldn't see her, but I heard her from where I sat on the loveseat inside our little living room, which looked directly out on the porch through a screen door. Whack. Whack. WHACK! went the rugs slamming against the banister. Snickers and derisive laughter wafted over from the Wisewurst's porch next door. When Mom came back inside, her voice and face clouded with hurt, rage and bewilderment, she said to my Dad, "Tom, they're doing it to spite me!"

My father said, "Soph, come on," and took her in his arms until her shoulders relaxed in his embrace, and she cried.

I respected my Dad for being loving and compassionate to Mom without being loud and ugly to the neighbors, whose snickering and mockery I hadn't noticed until Mom pointed it out. There were occasions when I would have loved to kick Mr. Wisewurst in the shin, but he wasn't worth thinking about twice. To be fair, Mom sometimes imagined slights, or made demands that were downright unreasonable and invited ridicule, like when she wanted to save the sidewalk pavements in front of our house to use as garden stones.

The city planned to replace the sidewalks, which didn't need replacing; they were one of the better things about our neighborhood. My brothers and I played running bases on these enormous slabs of smooth gray concrete, sometimes shaded light green with algae, but when dry, an inviting and lovely surface to draw on or play tic tac toe with a soft stone or chalk. These slabs of concrete measured approximately three by five feet, were six inches thick, and weighed close to a ton.

After the city dug them up, Mom asked the workers to leave the pavements where they were so we could haul them to the back yard. (Secretly she hoped they would offer to take them back behind our garage for her, but they didn't.) One summer evening, Mr. Wisewurst strolled out his front door and leaned up against his porch railing to watch the show, a wry grin on his face, as my father and I attempted to lift the slabs onto a Red Flyer wagon and transport them into our backyard. When we finally managed to hoist one cement slab onto the wagon, its wheels sank into the moist soil of our front lawn and wouldn't budge. Okay, so now we most definitely looked like Polacks screwing in a light bulb. But when Mom got an idea in her head, she simply wouldn't let it go. So I shouldn't blame Mr. Wisewurst too much for laughing at us, although I gave him the finger when my father wasn't looking, whereby he stormed into his house.

When I went to elementary school and John McBane told his Polish joke, I realized he was talking about me, us, my family. My highly classified mission was to keep the fact that I was half Polish utterly secret or else, I feared, I would become the butt of jokes. My classmates would have a field day with my Uncle Stanley, the accordion, Muma, Tutuh, and polkas. They'd rip me to shreds! But one day in Mrs. Harwood's fourth grade social studies class, we watched a film about immigrants arriving in the U.S. and passing through customs at Ellis Island. In the film, some American boys, pretending to be friendly, offered a Polish immigrant boy a banana, a fruit he'd never seen before. Then they laughed as the poor Polish boy bit into the banana, yellow peel and all, and made a horrible face. In turn, my whole class laughed at the Polish boy as children naturally do at someone else's misfortune, thereby cancelling out any lesson we might have learned from the film. I wondered if Mom or my Uncle Stanley had experienced something similar. As if reading my mind, Mrs. Harwood turned on the lights at the end of the film and asked, "Is anyone here Polish?"

I clenched my teeth to prevent my facial muscles from betraying me, to maintain the appearance that I was unruffled by the question, while my nervous system went on high alert, and I felt my heart pumping in my throat. I wanted to raise the top of my desk and hide under it, but my trusty friend Felicia pointed at me and said, "Annie is." Only then did I reluctantly raise my hand like a soldier volunteering to be the first to run through enemy fire, to admit I was Polish. Despite my efforts, my face began to do what it always did when I tried not to cry: crumple up like a discarded wad of paper. My classmates were staring at me since Mrs. Harwood's question still hung in the air, so the situation absolutely demanded that I appeared uninterested, indifferent. I nervously faked a giggle and poked Mary Clare Sweeney, the girl who sat in front of me, in the shoulder blade with my pencil eraser. Mary Clare turned around to look at me, eyebrows raised in question. I don't recall what Mrs. Harwood said or asked, or what I answered because it was all I could do to avoid fainting. I could only hear the rush of white noise filling my ears, feel the heat of shame on my neck, and I stared hard at Mary Clare Sweeney's broad face so I had something to focus on to keep from passing out. She must have been photogenic because the planes of Mary Clare's cheeks alone, not to mention the expanse of her forehead, nose, jutting chin, even her pores, were immense. She eyed me curiously, attempting to read just exactly what I was feeling, why I had poked her. I sensed an inkling that somehow I didn't fool her, that she read shame and embarrassment on my face. But she didn't know, how could she, being Irish herself, what this felt like. Did anyone ever make Irish jokes? I myself had never heard one. In our community, being Irish was celebrated on a special day every year, St. Patrick's Day, with a parade. Everyone wore green and drank green beer. No one ever had a St. Stanislaus Day with vodka and pierogies, at least no one that I knew of.

Pressure building in my chest threatened to push my heart out of my throat and become a sob. I hated being singled out in this way. I'd rather be a leper, have the cooties, or wet my pants in front of the whole class, but not be Polish; it was torture. I fought my emotions to keep my jaw in line, to keep my lips from turning down in a pout and quivering, to keep tears from spilling over onto my cheeks.

"I have to tell you something at recess," I whispered to the waiting Mary Clare, after what seemed like minutes but were really only seconds, and by then the class had lost interest. She smiled a wry, not unkind smile, then nodded and turned back around. The crisis was over. My classmates were busy taking out their spelling workbooks, and by the time the bell rang for recess, I invented some ruse to tell Mary Clare Sweeney.

No matter; all was forgotten due to the excitement created when Jeff Feder hurled a battle ball in the schoolyard and accidentally hit Mrs. Harwood, who was taking her turn for recess duty, in the head, knocking her out cold as she stood watching the boys play basketball.

Someone ran to get our principal, Sister Miriam Therese. I stood looking down at Mrs. Harwood, supine on the blacktop in her red woolen suit, her dark rimmed glasses knocked askew but still resting on the bridge of her nose, legs slightly but not indecently splayed, feet still in her sensible small black heels, her graying but neatly coiffed hair. She looked to be merely sleeping. Odd, to see a teacher in such a vulnerable position. I felt a certain detachment.

My gaze rested for a while on her face. I pitied her for being old, for certainly I would never be so old.

As I continued to stare, I was startled to see in her features traces of the beautiful young woman she once was.

THAT HOFFMAN GIRL

The first time I met Laurie Hoffman I was standing with my older brother John, waiting to pay for ice cream sundaes at Malley's. Laurie was working behind the glass cases, adding milk and dark chocolate bark to the trays on display. She wore the Malley's uniform, a green polyester dress, and had her honey blond hair drawn back and tied with a black ribbon. I admired the way she dignified the ugly uniform, but at the same time, my reaction to her perfection inspired a mischievousness in me, a need to destroy something. Perfect girls reminded me of my older sister, who seemed flawless in every way, and whose example I failed to follow. I winked at John, who had no idea what kind of crazy thing I might do on any given day, and muttered loud enough for Laurie to hear, "So *slow*…" as if commenting on the speed of her service. She heard me as I'd intended—her eyes widened, her mouth dropped open, and she said under her breath, "Ob*nox*ious!" I laughed, conveying, I thought, the idea that I was merely joking, and then she smiled. I don't know why I thought everyone should find me so funny, but I did. I could get away with it back then, I guess.

The next time I ran into Laurie was when we both tried out for a play at our high school. I was a sophomore, Laurie a junior. I was cast as the lead, a geisha girl named Lotus Blossom, and Laurie got the part of an old Japanese refugee woman leaving Okinawa, with just one line. I don't remember ever looking back at where Laurie sat behind me backstage, through all our many rehearsals, on a huge wagon piled with what were supposed to be her life's belongings. The fact that I only realize this now horrifies me. She had to sit through that whole first act with one line at the end! I was too preoccupied with the business of *my* Japanese lines and a few awkward moments with Kevin Quimby, who played an American soldier.

I was surprised when Laurie invited me to get coffee with her. One Saturday afternoon she picked me up in a vintage burgundy Cadillac convertible with cream-colored leather seats. I felt stunned to be the object of her attention, especially since she was older than me. Her car impressed me, but at the time I didn't realize how just the appearance of that Cadillac on my street would make people look up and take note.

We went to a place called Beachcliffe, a little mall over the border of Lakewood in Rocky River, for coffee and ice cream. We talked and talked. It turned out we attended the same church.

"Doesn't your brother play guitar at the Saturday Mass?"

I'd never seen Laurie at our church before, although she wasn't easy to miss. She stood six feet tall, something she lamented because boys were always shorter than her. Anyone would have found that awkward. She was beautiful, with a broad luminous face that I knew would photograph well. She could have been a model. Her blond hair framed her cheeks and ended just under her chin. Her wide hazel eyes stared out at me from a slightly freckled complexion. She always looked a little astonished, but she wasn't a ditz. She took the hardest math and science classes they offered at our high school.

Still, I felt a need to guard myself around Laurie. What I mean is, I couldn't be entirely honest with her because I soon found out that I came from a very different home than she did. She was the youngest of two children, and her older brother had just left for college, so she was the only one left at home. She lived in a bigger house than ours, not a mansion, but a more respectable house in terms of the hierarchy of houses in my hometown of Lakewood. Another reason I felt guarded around her was because I quickly learned I'd had more experiences, however innocent, with boys, and because we were both Catholic, I didn't know if she would disapprove of me as a sinner, or whatever we called it back then, even though I wasn't a "sinner" in the sexual sense that the Catholic church defined. Still, I often felt like a sinner anyway. The all pervasive guilt—any Catholic knows what I mean. Once, when we were talking about boys, Laurie asked me a question.

"If you knew you were going to die in a few days, would you have sex with like, say, your boyfriend? Or say Kevin Quimby." Kevin Quimby played the American soldier in "Teahouse." He and Lotus Blossom had a little thing.

"I don't know...." I said reluctantly. *Definitely*, I thought.

"Anne..." Laurie shook her head.

"Huh?"

"We have to be strong."

"Oh. Yeah."

I was a virgin and already feeling guilty about sex I hadn't had yet? My dishonesty with Laurie made me feel uncomfortable, with her, with myself, I wasn't sure.

I didn't envy Laurie's car, although I admired and coveted her clean, well-ordered home with a mother who was there to give us sandwiches one day. Her mother barely spoke. She wore a dress, and an apron in the kitchen. It seemed to me she moved through the rooms of her well-kept, hushed house with quiet grace. She wasn't totally bogged down with young ones and housework like my mother. I thought to myself once how our family could have used the space in Laurie's house. But we would have ruined it in no time.

Laurie's bedroom called to mind a feature from *Seventeen Magazine*, to which I had become a subscriber using my birthday money, in the heyday of Phoebe Cates. Oak wood floors, covered in a few places with plush white rugs, glowed golden in the sunlight that streamed into the second story room from two crystal clear windows, expertly curtained and valanced in white eyelet. A queen sized bed, Laurie didn't have to share with anyone else; a vertically slender-slatted white wood headboard, covered with a chic quilt in pink and cream. Ruffled shams. The whitest of white clean sheets beneath. I wondered how it might feel to slide into those sheets, in that room, alone and quiet. The freshness and beauty of Laurie's bedroom enchanted me. I didn't try to explain this to her, but I knew I could never show her where I slept. In fact I was afraid to ask her over to my house. I was always afraid to ask friends over to my house, all except for Trudy Zimmer, the Giamatti's, and Jenny Zickes, who considered our family civilized in comparison to hers.

The day her mother made us cucumber and chicken salad sandwiches on white bread from which she'd removed the crusts, Laurie told me a secret. Swept away a bit, feeling as if I suddenly inhabited a world I'd never known existed, I didn't pay close attention to her disclosure at the time. How was it that I could live to the age of fifteen and not know people lived in such splendor and refinement?

After we ate and took our plates to the sink, she led me through some swinging doors to a plushly carpeted dining room. A wooden sideboard, polished to a reflective shine, ran along one wall parallel to the dining table, with a set of shelves on each side of a central cabinets. Laurie opened the cabinet and removed a folder. From the folder she carefully withdrew an 8x10 picture. Perhaps a high school portrait, of a beautiful young woman with jet black hair and an even paler complexion than Laurie's. Her green eyes regarded us with as haughty an expression as the portrait of Rebecca in the movie version of Daphne du Maurier's book. (I had happened to see it because I liked Alfred Hitchcock movies.) She seemed to be laughing at us, or at everything in general. I knew that expression. I sometimes used it, too, but I didn't look anything like the young woman in the photo. Neither did Laurie.

"I have to tell you something, but it's kind of a secret," Laurie whispered. "This is my sister Claire. We don't talk about her."

"Why not?"

"She's...she isn't like us," she said. "I mean, she's really smart and everything, but it's like she has no conscience and does all kinds of bad things."

"Like what?"

"Well, she takes drugs and tries to use my parents to get money. When she comes around, she brings her boyfriend and talks like she's a black person. It's really weird."

"Why does she do that? Talk like a black person, I mean."

"I don't know. I mean, she actually *sounds* black."

"Wow." I didn't know what else to say. I guessed it would be odd to see and hear a white person trying to sound black.

Laurie put the picture of her sister back in the cabinet and I forgot about what she told me almost immediately, so there was never any need for her to fear my telling her family's secret.

She graduated from high school and went away to Ohio State. On her return home for Christmas break she asked if she could visit me. She had a gift for me, she said, and arrived at my house at about 11 a.m. on a Saturday morning. I asked her to come in and sit in our little living room to talk. I knew it wasn't the best time. Not only were things typically tense between me and my mother, but Saturday was cleaning and grocery day, and luckily I had already cleaned the bathroom, dusted and vacuumed from the upstairs hall, down the stairs, into the living room. My mother had just returned from the store and was in the kitchen unloading everything while simultaneously cooking lunch. Laurie sat down on our couch and gave me a wrapped package—which turned out to be a t-shirt from Ohio State. She didn't much like it there, she said, because it was too big and classes were so large, sometimes they taught them on television monitors in huge auditoriums.

Five feet away from us, my little brothers fought and cried at the dining room table—they were probably hungry. Suddenly my mother yelled at them in a tone of voice I recognized as a warning sign. How can I describe the sound of someone driven to the limits of their patience? Shrieking is what it sounded like to Laurie. I knew it as a sound that evoked in me both compassion and fear. I glanced at Laurie, who looked over my head and flinched. My mother, though only 10 feet away, was hidden behind the doorway to the kitchen. I'll never forget how Laurie then looked at me, her eyes widened in horror and fear, and with a sort of question. I assumed she'd never before heard anyone scream like that when it was a common occurrence in our house.

I recall my own reaction: resignation. What could I do? How could I explain how things were to Laurie? I wasn't really ashamed. I returned her look, mine expressionless, only my eyes imploring her to understand.

I couldn't take her up to a room I shared with my little sister because then she'd see that 3 of my little brothers were crammed into the other room, three twin beds in a row without any space between them, my parents in a third room, and this was with 3 of my siblings away at college.

I wasn't afraid for her to see it. I wasn't really embarrassed, but I knew it would shock her. So I said nothing. After a few more moments of listening to my mother screaming at my brothers, (and I have to say, I began to suspect that my mother did this on purpose to spite me) I was relieved when Laurie made an excuse to leave. We got up, I said goodbye and thanked her, and she left.

I went to the kitchen to help my mother with lunch. I wanted to ask her why...why did she make things so difficult for me? But at that moment I felt I knew she would try to ruin anything good that could or would happen to me. Anything that would let me rise above what we were, what she was, whatever *that* meant, I didn't even know. She didn't seem to have this problem with my other seven siblings, though. She confirmed my suspicions when, wiping her wet hands on a dish towel, she said, "Is she that Hoffman girl? She's *boring*," as if to justify her behavior. Was she jealous?

Although we always argued, this time I didn't say anything. Maybe my mother was right, maybe Laurie was a little boring despite her car and her nice bedroom. Still. She liked me. I mean, I think my Mom thought no one liked me. Or maybe she thought I was getting too big for my britches. It had happened before. Once when I was in eighth grade, my whole class stopped talking to me because I was "going with" a boy from the public school, and they found me conceited, among other things. I had felt traumatized.

I saw less and less of Laurie after that. We still talked and went out to get coffee occasionally, but she began to hang out with two of the most popular girls from her class who also lived in Lakewood, close to the lake. The Swensen Twins, we called them, Mattie and Missie. They were naturally beautiful and sincerely nice, as wholesome as models from the Wrigley's Doublemint Chewing Gum commercials.

The last time I saw Laurie was about 20 years ago. Apparently one of the Swensen twins, I could never keep them straight, had moved near to where I lived. I was still young and thin, and had gone out with my husband and some friends. We sat talking and drinking wine on the patio of the Blind Lemon, a cafe in Mt. Adams, when I noticed not Laurie, but the Swensen twins. Then I saw Laurie, who didn't appear to recognize or remember me, or to disapprove of something, about how I looked. Embarrassed, in my discomfort, I made a joke that really made no sense at all.

I said to everyone in general of my old friend Laurie, "She knew me when I was a good little girl." What the hell did *that* mean, exactly? Laurie and the twin made little comment, but smiled and were cordial. I have always regretted saying that, because once again, it wasn't honest. I wasn't a good little girl. Nor was I a bad girl. Why did I do and say such stupid things?

I liked Laurie. I just didn't feel I could be myself around her, was all. That required good behavior, which I wasn't prone to all the time.

When I think of that scene at the Blind Lemon, I still cringe. If I saw her today, I'd say, "Laurie, it's wonderful to see you again. I've thought of you often over the years."